Rolling in the Mud

Kelly Van Nelson is a contemporary author and poet from Newcastle-upon-Tyne, now living in Australia. Her poems, short stories and articles have featured in numerous international publications and she regularly appears on radio and television discussing current issues prevalent in society. She is represented by the Newman Agency.

Graffiti Lane, her powerful debut poetry collection, showcased at the London Book Fair and became an instant bestseller, raising awareness and influencing change around bullying, domestic violence, mental health, and suicide. *Punch and Judy*, her second #1 bestselling poetry collection, puts the spotlight on domestic violence, generating much needed conversation. Her books have been gifted to television celebrities, music icons and A-list Hollywood Oscar nominees and winners.

Kelly is the recipient of a KSP First Edition Fellowship, an AusMumpreneur 'Big Idea – Changing the World' Gold Award winner for her creative use of the literary word as an antibullying advocate, a double Roar Success Award winner for Best Book (Graffiti Lane) and Most Powerful Influencer, a Telstra Business Women's Award and a 2020 CEO Magazine Managing Director of the Year Finalist.

Kelly is the mum of two children, wife of her soulmate of more than two decades and managing director on the executive board of a Fortune 500. In the spare time she doesn't have, you can find her hanging out on the open mic performing poetry. In short, she is a juggler.

www.kellyvannelson.com

Also by Kelly Van Nelson

Graffiti Lane

Graffiti Lane Collector's Edition

Punch and Judy

Kelly Van Nelson

Rolling in the Mud

For Roy and Sandra
who blessed my world
with faith and family

Rolling in the Mud
ISBN 978 1 76109 038 7

Cover photo by Tim Mossholder on Unsplash

First published 2020 by
GINNINDERRA PRESS
PO Box 3461 Port Adelaide 5015
www.ginninderrapress.com.au

Contents

No Need For Speed

The pungent stench of marijuana clings to my nostrils. I suck in deep breaths, trying to get high from passive smoking. Dad grows his own weed that I'm not allowed to touch, since I'm not sick like he is. Brain as sharp as a dope needle, but multiple sclerosis has possessed his body, ramming into him with zero respect for personal space. A year ago, he was considered a hero, putting out fires and rescuing cats from trees. Now people look away when I push him around in his wheelchair. Nobody can see the incredible man concealed behind a curtain of muscle spasms.

I haul myself out of bed, stoked there's no college today. Sun's up and it's a ripper for some gnarly skateboard action at the bowl. My favourite black T-shirt is in a rumpled heap on the floor next to the PlayStation controller. Washing machine packed in last month and been hand washing since, so all my clothes are a bit sketchy. I pick it up and give it a sniff. Good enough to survive another wear since it's only gonna get sweaty. I pull it on and give my hair a ruffle. Crying out for a decent cut, otherwise I'll be needing an elastic soon to keep it out the way. Teeth can wait. I'll brush them when I get back.

The pint glass on my desk is almost full. Been saving to replace my ancient wheel bearings with Bones Super Swiss. They're the fastest around, period. A winning pre-lubricated combo of precision ground and polished races. I pull out the notes, count, and shove them in the back pocket of my jeans. Just enough to buy essential groceries, plus the skateboard bearings. Dad can't work any more and it's been rough since the big C gave Mum a fatal coward's punch out of nowhere.

I grab my board and head down the passage, pausing to check on Dad. He's snoring in bed, same position I left him in last night. Sleeps late most days.

Outside, I feel the buzz as I do an acid drop off the porch stairs. I warm up in the drive, doing ollies and kickflips with decent pop. I lean back on my tail, let the board kick up, catch it with a pendulum swing, then straight back on, right foot forward, Goofy. Birds chirp as I hit the street. Not much other noise except the friction of my wheels on pavement. It's a clean run to the park. Nobody around to see me land a sick 540 on the half pipe.

I manage an hour before a huge gang arrives. They ignore me and herd into the bowl, slow grazing the ramps like they're made of grass, not concrete. One of them sparks a joint, grazing on a different kind of grass. Suspect he's not smoking for medicinal purposes. An impatient dude snakes me, dropping in before it's his turn. I don't bother mentioning he might wanna wait in line. Ignorant poser can have it. I rehydrate at the water fountain and head to the mall.

Metal shutters are still down when I get to the skate shop. I lean against the wall opposite and check them out. They've been sprayed with killer graffiti, professionally done to incorporate designer-brand advertising. Thrasher decorates the front of a skater's cap and the Santa Cruz logo is prominent everywhere else. Sick art work. The security guard walks past me three times. I probably look dodgy, loitering here, but it doesn't take a genius to see I've a bulky board in my hands, so I'm hardly going to embark on a snatch and run.

The sound of metal grating on the runners is better than the Foo Fighters to my ears. The shutters roll up and I'm first in.

'Want any help?' a pretty brunette asks.

I pretend I don't know what I'm looking for, so she gives me the low-down on the equipment on the racks. I try not to stare at her rack. Been a while since I broke up with Cheryl and I probably should get back on the circuit.

They've got the bearings I'm after in stock. One pack left.

'Popular,' says the hot shop assistant, catching my line of sight. 'You should buy them. Might be a while before we get more stock delivered.'

I stick my hand in my back pocket and curl my fingers around the notes. When my hand comes out, it's empty. 'Might pop back next week.'

She looks disappointed as I walk away. Part of me is too, but shit happens.

Supermarket is open. I stick my board in the trolley and wander the aisles, packing the same old staples around it: bread, milk, mince. I'm a total pro at making various dishes out of minced beef. Bolognese, lasagne, chili con carne, beef and bean cowboy pot. MasterChef, eat your heart out.

When I get to the confectionery aisle, I splurge on a box of Ferrero Rocher. Dad loves the things. I pay the cashier with the notes from my back pocket and squeeze my grocery stash into one carrier bag, then nip in the bottle store to buy a bottle of Johnny Walker.

I skate home; no tricks. Don't want to topple and have the booze crash in the gutter.

'Hey, Nick,' Dad yells when I come in the front door.

I go to his bedroom and prop him up on the pillows. He looks pale; thinner than yesterday.

'Got you some goodies.' I unpack the shopping. When I put the whisky and chocolates on the bedside table, his eyes fill up.

'You shouldn't have spent your money on me, son. I thought you were going to upgrade your skateboard. I'm looking forward to seeing you master more tricks.'

'Plenty of time, Dad. Plenty of time.'

My throat catches. We both know it's a lie. Doctor's given him three months max. Wheel bearings that speed up life can wait. Right now, all I want is to slow death down.

Solo

Bernard watched the hands of his antique grandfather clock slowly move. The pain seared his heart with every tick. Time healed nothing, but it did bring him closer to Violet.

He remembered meeting her for the first time, at the church dinner dance. The red lipstick mark left on the thinly sliced white bread when she took a bite of her cucumber sandwich. The way her face had lit up his world with a smile when she'd caught him staring at her. It was not the smile of a stranger, but one filled with warmth and promise. Women usually sent him spiralling into a nervous state, but not this pretty brunette, with the slender figure and the endearing mole on her right cheek. She'd had the opposite effect on him, compelling him to ask her to dance. Her hand had taken his. It was as delicate as the bone china the diners supped their tea from. A melody played on the gramophone, courtesy of Louis Armstrong. It was one of his best.

Bernard loved brass band entertainment and Armstrong was a genius; so much so, his music had managed to filter its way from America to England. Bernard loved how Armstrong had an ability to seamlessly shift the mix of the sound from an impressive trumpet solo performance to a collective improvisation with fellow jazz musicians. It lifted his spirits in a time when war savagely ripped away everything else.

A whirlwind romance progressed and within a month they were sharing Sunday cream cakes with his mother.

It was a three-tier fruit cake the following year, iced in cream cheese and buttermilk, with lilac flowers pouring down the layers like a waterfall. Violet whispered her vows to Bernard from behind a lace white veil, her voice low and husky. The longest of eyelashes framed her deep green eyes and the perfect oval of her face gave her an ethereal beauty that left him breathless. They spent the night at the local inn on the edge of the estate, unable to afford a honeymoon further afield. Their room had been in the attic. The centrepiece was a soft double bed with matching bedside lamps either side, decorated with burgundy tassels.

'Wow, you booked the penthouse,' Violet murmured in his ear.

'One day, after the war is over, we'll go away on a proper honeymoon.'

'This is perfect, Bernard.'

He loved her positive attitude. Even though they were on the top floor, the noise from the rowdy clientele in the bar downstairs still drifted up the wooden staircase. The place was popular with local men who liked to play cards and drink too much. Violet deserved so much more than this.

As if sensing his concern, Violet reached out and cupped his face in her hands, kissing him deeply. When her fingers began to trace down his body, he'd almost combusted. Passion took over and their bodies effortlessly moulded into one another. He had walked with a bounce in his step for weeks afterwards.

When Violet told him she was pregnant, Bernard had foolishly wondered how they would make ends meet. The first words that spilled from his mouth were 'Times are gonna be hard, chicken.'

Usually she smiled when he fondly referred to her after the chicks they kept in the backyard of her parents' house where they lived, but this time a shadow crossed her face. He bitterly regretted not pausing to think before he had spoken. Such a shame hindsight couldn't be bottled and sold along with silk stockings; an aid like that, for men needing help in treating a lady like a queen, would fly off the shelves. If only he could turn the hands of their old grandfather clock back, Bernard would have changed every one of those moments where he failed to love and cherish Violet like there was no tomorrow.

The warmongering of the Germans brought hardship on the population of Britain. Violet lost her job in the tea room where she worked as a waitress and Bernard had his shifts at the factory halved. London went underground into shelters made for trains. Bernard desperately wanted to go underground with Violet too, but Neville Chamberlain backed every fit and healthy man into a corner and imposed conscription upon them all.

Violet had hugged the breath out of him the day he left for the army training camp. 'Promise you won't make me one of those people who receives a telegram bearing bad news.'

'I promise.'

*

He'd never thought to make her promise the same thing in return. He was in the trenches, knee-deep in mud, when he received the darkest news that disease had taken her. His heart broke in half, one side for Chicken and the other for their unborn child. His telegram said they had been buried in a quiet graveyard not far from their home and were at peace together. At least they had each other. Bernard had not been there for them in death, just as he was not there for them in life.

It was impossible to mourn such a catastrophic loss. His eyes remained dry and his gun fully loaded. Bernard hid his grief under the harsh material of his khaki uniform and went back into battle. He knew combat on the front line was the quickest way to join his beloved family in heaven.

*

The war was cruel in so many ways. Millions of innocent lives lost, yet Bernard managed to survive two bullets, gangrene of the leg, and a case of tuberculosis. Fearless in his fighting, he was first to charge into every battle, craving his own death as much as that of the enemy.

Medals decorated his uniform, but they felt cold to the touch. All he wanted was to be encased in the warmth of a wooden coffin next to Violet and their baby. Bernard was no hero. He was just a solo trumpeter without a brass band.

Another One Bites the Dust

A layer of red dust coated his tan boots, far thicker than icing sugar sprinkled on a Victoria sponge. His feet were sweating inside the clunky steel cap lace-ups. He wore thick woollen socks with the aim of giving some relief to the blisters on his heels that came from gruelling twelve-hour shifts. Normally he couldn't wait to clock off. He liked to take the fastest route from the mine site to his donger, where he usually tore off the high-vis shirt, the cotton drill cargo pants, and the monstrous footwear, to scrub his skin clean under the trickle that masqueraded as a shower. But not tonight.

Tonight, Miles strolled slowly towards the burnt orange sun that hovered in brutal stubbornness as it resisted the moment it would have to disappear off the north-west shelf of Australia. The sunset was breathtaking, but the starkness of the vast land around him had a beauty to it that had been marred the instant deposits of metal had been identified in sedimentary rocks. Specialists had swarmed in, churning out their environmental studies so they could best advise the mining moguls on how to sensitively excavate at a price per tonne that could sustain the volatile stock market. An aesthetically ugly wind turbine and solar farm had sprung up, the renewable energy source designed to mitigate the hikes in keeping diesel fuel generators topped up. Roads were carved through the bush, scattering wildlife to allow connectivity to the remotest of areas. The displacement of indigenous communities from land they traditionally owned sickened him too, but what turned his stomach more was he'd muscled in on the action and had been making a living on the mines for the last two decades.

Every few minutes, he paused to swipe away a fly from his bearded face. The sound of the ocean could be heard in the distance. Sometimes he wished he could wade into the waves, to let the icy needles numb his pain and the riptide pull him out along with the cracked shells. The only reason he hadn't taken the plunge was because with his rotten luck he'd wash up alive and well on the Pilbara coast; a message in a bottle, announcing his failure for the entire crew to laugh at.

The construction workers were a nasty bunch. They called him Tarantula, constantly sniggering at his long legs. Today, when he was conducting safety checks on the erecting of the scaffolding, he'd been subjected to worse than the usual four-letter insults.

'I bet he harnesses the legs of his missus in the air just to get some action,' Charlie, the construction supervisor mocked.

He had ignored the ripple of laughter among the crew working on the new accommodation block that was being hailed as the FIFO Four Seasons. It was destined to replace the ancient dongas that were probably riddled with asbestos. With a pool, gym, and unlimited Netflix, it would be luxury for the fly-in-fly-out workers just like him, who did their stint to pay for private school for the kids and weekly gel nails and designer haircuts for the wife back in Perth. Miles had kept his head down and checked the karabiners that were the connection point between Charlie's harness and the lanyard into the fixed anchor point. When they'd interviewed him for the site safety manager position, Westerhope Mining Corporation had been very specific about their low tolerance levels towards unnecessary deaths. It was his job to keep the bullying pricks alive.

'Hurry the fuck up, Tarantula,' Charlie had sneered. 'Friction from your curly mop is causing a hole in the ozone layer.'

For a split second, Miles had considered unhooking the karabiner. He'd badly wanted to push Charlie over the edge of the scaffolding so he could watch his smug head smash open like a pumpkin. Instead, he'd carried on with his work, checking the various connections, the suitability of the personal protective equipment, and the work at heights permits validity for the zillionth time. Miles, if nothing else, was efficient, thorough and reliable. He was safe hands.

The chaffing from the boots was almost unbearable. He used to slap Band-Aids on his feet until one of the blokes saw him buy a multipack in the general store and told the whole crew what a pussy he was. His blisters had been raw ever since.

A storage structure was visible a kilometre or so away. It was nothing more than a sloped sheet of corrugated metal propped up by four wooden pillars. Abandoned machinery was parked underneath; the shell of a forklift truck, an old bobcat and a minibus that had lost its dignity when someone stripped off its wheels. Miles often took sanctuary in the shack to escape the racket he was subjected to in his donger that had walls so thin he could hear the guys housed on either side of him jerking off. He picked up pace, desperate for solitude. Minutes later, he was under cover, scrambling up the front of the mini bus and onto its rusty roof. He sat down and shrugged off his backpack, filled with safety equipment, sun lotion and an empty water bottle. He shoved the bag behind his back to prop himself up.

As nightfall crept in, a stridulation of crickets began to build into a crescendo. Miles admired how thousands of crickets all rubbed their upper and lower wings together in such harmony while the humans in this place struggled to co-exist. Their chirping, coupled with the background noise of the tide, was a comforting lullaby, making Miles close his eyes.

He lay for a long time, until the dry air cooled and his arms began to develop goosebumps under the fluorescent yellow of his sleeves. When he opened his eyes, they were filled with tears and the sky enveloping him was dark. Clouds shrouded the moon and the rumbling of thunder warned of rain. Miles loved the Pilbara weather, but tonight, even the promise of a tropical storm did nothing to appease his anxiety. The squeeze of his heart was intense, and he gulped in air, hyperventilating, gasping, struggling to satisfy the needs of his lungs.

He thought of his teenage sons. The eldest was about to graduate Year Twelve with straight As, giving him a golden ticket into the University of Western Australia. The youngest, a tearaway with an attitude, had his heart set on becoming a plumber. Even in his lowest moments of depression, he loved his boys, but he couldn't remember the last time they'd needed him.

His weeping grew louder until great racking sobs rattled his ribcage. Just like his boys, his wife also managed just fine when he was away, changing plugs and making stews in the slow cooker. When he was home, she complained about the disruption to her routine and they typically fought until he sought solace in a six-pack. The love in their relationship had flown from the domestic departure lounge too many times for her to care about him any more, but he regretted not spending more time with his children. He should have been around to light the barbecue and take them to a cricket game, but it was too late now. The sausages were charred black and their cricketing heroes were nothing but a bunch of disgraced cheaters.

He sat up and dragged his backpack around to unzip it, then shone his phone torch on its contents while he rummaged around. The coil of bumblebee rope he pulled out was made of yellow and black, triple-strand, intertwined PolyPRO, designed with UV resistance and guaranteed to minimise abrasions. Since it was the dead of night, the UV resistance feature was wasted, but an irrational part of his brain told him that taking the sting out of enduring painful abrasions was worth paying a premium for.

He unravelled the rope and used his penknife to cut the length he needed, then he pushed himself onto his knees and placed the rope in front of him. His fingers, usually so nimble, fumbled as he formed a letter C, then a letter S, with a long lead at one end. He compressed all three strands of the S together, pinching them so the ends fanned out in a bow tie, then he wrapped the original end of the C shape around and around, leaving a loop to pull the end string through. He pulled the noose closed and tightened his handiwork before standing to pull it over his head.

The ceiling above him was low enough to reach. He used the harness from his bag to secure himself onto the rafters. Using a karabiner and his tarantula limbs, he crawled, along the underside of the roof, until he reached the highest point of the structure. The irony of paying attention to safety in a moment like this was not lost on him, but the last thing he wanted was to tumble to the ground and break a leg, or worse, his spine. The palms of his hands were damp as he hooked the bumblebee rope around the rafter and made some final adjustments.

His colleagues were relentless bullies. Big bullies with small minds, who undermined his authority, verbally abused him at every opportunity, and spat in his tea when they thought he wasn't looking. He'd reported them more than once, but nobody cared a damn about the muscle flexing going on. The moguls needed the Four Seasons built so the masses could swoop in to dig the iron ore out of the ground. They'd have another hole to dig now too; one that wouldn't require any turbo powered tools. It would be small enough to manually excavate with a shovel, which would keep the environmentalists happy.

Charlie unclipped the karabiner on his harness and let himself fall until his boots swung just above the red earth. When the night was over, they'd find him and ship his body out of here on the first available flight. Fly-in-fly-out. Another one bites the dust.

Mining was all he knew, and he knew too much. He'd allowed his morals to be cloaked in the madness of the money. His soul would remain here, a glitch on the clean slate of death statistics. Zero tolerance, they'd said. Now he was their Pilbara ghost. Punishing the bullies at dawn, haunting them at dusk.

Doves Fly

The music is so loud nobody speaks. We communicate through movement. Hands waving in the air to the latest Garage House hit.

You happy?

Yeah, me too.

I've got fluorescent bands on both wrists. No chance you'll lose me tonight.

The club stinks. Sweat from bodies jammed in to jam to the beat. Disinfectant mixed with the aroma of stale vomit. Love it – the smell of freedom. There's no better place to run away from reality. Turned eighteen last week. Mum can't stop me partying now. Getting so much wear out of these tight denim hotpants. Kept the midriff bare. Thinking about getting my bellybutton pierced like Jody's. She looks hot tonight. Might kiss her. Nah, she's got her tongue down some random bloke's throat.

You happy, Jody?

The beat changes. Nightcrawlers, 'Push the Feeling On'. Killer track. I tug off one of the pink fluorescent bands and use it to pull my hair back from my flushed face. Tie it up high; high is good. I cut some pulsing moves. My ass wiggles low, then back up with a sashay of the hips. Downers and uppers. Dancing is everything. Fills the soul with rich meaning. Graduated school last week. They don't teach you about nightclubbing in class. Dunno why. Learned more about myself in here than I ever did in front of a blackboard. Found my deepest self. What makes me tick. How fast my head spins. The buzz of a racing heart.

I nip to the toilet. Queue is longer than the Great Wall. Put on some cherry blossom lippy as I wait my turn. The lips still feel dry. Mouth too. I step out of line and use my hands to cup water from the tap. Gulp it down before some irate chick snakes me into a cubicle. Relieved to make it to the front unscathed and lock myself inside. Rummage in my silver clutch for another white pill. Ecstasy. Third of the night. Should keep me going until morning. It has a dove imprint on one side. Doves make you fly higher than anything else being pushed by the dealers. Pop it in my mouth and head back to the dance floor.

Feel free. Feel good. Feel thirsty.

I topple over. The floor is sticky. My face is stuck on it. Head is so heavy. So many feet around me. Disco lights blur. Just the one blue light flashing. Fluorescent band is swapped for a medical band. Blackout.

There is a chance you might lose me tonight after all.

Cold Turkey

It had been ten years since he sipped a drink, but the memory of whisky caressing his tongue remained. Strange how he'd never considered himself an alcoholic until he quit drinking. Even the sherry trifle and brandy pudding, both of which his mother slaved over for Christmas desserts, wouldn't pass his lips. He'd told her about omitting liquor from her cooking, but she couldn't resist adding a splash. She was clattering pots in the kitchen, getting ready to bring out the final *pièce de résistance*: gravy made from red wine. He'd have to manoeuvre carefully around the food to avoid hurting her feelings.

Roast potatoes on a platter could not distract him from the dead bird they garnished; hot turkey legs trussed up in string and stuffed in between. His stomach churned. Hot turkey while on a cold turkey diet! It wasn't his mother's fault. She certainly didn't mean to rub his nose in it. Everything these days made him think about alcohol.

The tinsel wreath hanging above the mantlepiece winked, sparkling with happiness at being allowed out of the attic for the festive season. Better to look at such decorations, he supposed, than being buried six feet under a funeral wreath because he'd drunk himself to death.

*

Absconding from alcohol had been the result of a wrong office party a decade ago. He'd been dancing with his wife, Christine, to upbeat music from an enthusiastic Latin band. Alex couldn't tear his eyes from her. She looked like an angel, red curls loosely piled on her head, translucent skin, and cheekbones you could ski down. The cut of her green velvet dress accentuated the contours of her body, begging him to pull her close. They'd spent a fortune paying a bloke in tight trousers and shiny shoes to teach them the salsa. The result was a synchronised couple with effortless rhythm that no doubt had the whole room watching them in envy.

'Let's get out of here,' Christine whispered as the tune ended.

'Something wrong with my moves?'

'Nope. In fact, I was hoping to see more of them in private.'

'Sold.' He knew from the glow on her face she was going to make leaving the party early worthwhile.

Her hand squeezed his as they weaved their way towards the door.

'Alex, where have you been hiding,' a voice boomed as they passed a table littered with empty beer bottles. It was Mandelson hollering, the prick of a boss who regularly set impossible targets.

'On the dance floor.'

'Have a drink on me,' said Mandelson.

'It's an open bar.'

'Even better,' Mandelson guffawed.

'We were just leaving.'

'Nonsense. One for the road. Your lovely wife won't mind you sharing a Cuban cigar and nightcap with your manager, do you, doll?'

Alex looked sheepishly at Christine. 'Just one more, I promise.'

*

Christine was gone when the haze of Mandelson's cigar smoke cleared. She'd never learned to drive and wouldn't brave the Underground late at night, so Alex figured she'd taken a taxi home. He wanted to feel her breathing down his neck, nagging him to leave while he was still sober enough to drive her home, but he massaged away the knots of guilt. Another dram with coke. A double on the rocks. Mandelson was regaling a story about some secretary he'd nailed last Christmas after she offered him a sweet mince pie. Alex felt his head spin. He pushed himself up and staggered past Mandelson.

'Where are you going, son? I was just getting to the juicy bit where she dropped her pink lace pants.'

Alex wanted to point out he'd been nobody's son since his dad died of liver failure the day before Alex was due to celebrate his ninth birthday with new Lego and a chocolate cake, but he bit his tongue. Nobody wanted to hear a sob story, least of all Mandelson.

He stumbled outside. As he pulled the car keys from the pocket of his jacket, he realised how thankful he was to have a woman like Christine in his life. She wore pink lace underwear too sometimes, but he never aired the linen in public.

In the parking lot, he noticed too late the lady in the green velvet dress stepping in front of his car. The bang sobered Alex up instantly.

*

He'd found out later Christine had been in the bathroom, being comforted by a work colleague. When she came out, Mandelson was alone nursing a tipple and Christine had run outside looking for Alex.

He got out of the car and collapsed on the road, cradling her until his clothing was soaked red and the emergency services arrived to pry him away.

*

Alex pulled a cracker with his mother and forced a laugh as she read the lousy joke that fell out about a seagull and a man called Cliff. No point making his mother miserable on Christmas Day too.

He tugged on a green paper party hat. Tears sprang to his eyes as the image of Christine in her green dress sprang to mind again. He'd done jail time, paying for the consequences of drink driving, but it should have been the death penalty. He'd taken the life of a beautiful woman who brought so much joy to the world. Getting off the booze had been a rollercoaster. Part of him wanted to drink hooch with the other inmates to eclipse the ache in his heart. In the end, he'd done what was right. Punished himself with a sobriety life sentence. Some called whisky 'sweet nectar', but Alex knew the devil was hidden behind the black label.

Lunch was quickly cooling, so he shovelled a slice of meat into his mouth. He swallowed without chewing and dry-retched.

One way or another, cold turkey was going to kill him.

Deathly Silence

It was a stiff walk uphill to the graveyard. Celeste was glad she'd worn her new sneakers under her black jeans so she could tackle the distance at a brisk speed. Despite her pace, she still took care to ensure she stepped in the centre of every paving stone. She'd once read somewhere that misfortune and bad luck could be brought upon anyone stupid enough to tread on the cracks. Evil superstitions were not to be sniffed at on Halloween.

She wished it was a cooler night, cloaked by a howling wind or a thunderous rain storm that would wash away her sins and turn her lips blue. Halloween was meant to be cold and dark. Such an occasion simply did not warrant this dry Perth weather. The Australian sun hovered to the west, clinging on stubbornly to the final moments of dusk, even though a huge full moon was trying to muscle in above the rooftops to the east.

'Jeremy' by Pearl Jam pumped through her earphones. Eddie Vedder throwing a dope eternal punch on behalf of a fifteen-year-old sophomore from Texas that he'd read about in the newspaper. With a helping hand from a Smith and Wesson, the boy checked out in front of an audience of his schoolmates. Celeste didn't like to think too much about what could possibly drive a kid to put a Magnum revolver in his mouth and pull the trigger in second period English class, but the lyrics were killer.

Even though a damp patch of perspiration was beginning to form on her lower back, she pulled the hood of her black sweater over her low blonde ponytail. Regardless of the weather, she liked wearing thick, baggy clothing, with at least one pocket for her iPhone. She cranked up the volume on her device while she cut through the heart of the suburb. She lived just over thirty kilometres south of the city centre in a lacklustre, single-storey structure, with 'No Junk' scrawled on the mail box, mocking the pile of rusting junk in her driveway that was made up of everything from an old wheelbarrow to her broken first bike. She past several other similar properties built on small blocks of land, most with rickety wooden verandas running along the front. A few were the homes of students from her high school, most of whom shared the freedom of having parents who let them roam around way past dark and never smelled their breath for traces of alcohol.

She wondered which of the usual suspects would be at the meeting spot tonight, behind the cluster of tombstones that were all from the same family, by the name of Williamson, who died over a century ago. It was the perfect setting for the occasion. If the crumbling slabs above ground were anything to judge by, the skeletons buried six feet under must be in a hellish state. Halloween or no Halloween, Ella and Lucy would be there for sure. They had promised to bring their eldest sister's Ouija board. Usually, they were also armed with a couple of Pilsner tinnies pilfered from their pergola bar fridge, which made them two of her besties. They were fourteen, just like Celeste, but while she was an only child, they were identical twins with three older sisters and a boring half-brother who owned golf clubs and could well have been born sometime before the first ever gold prospector put a shovel into the Australian earth.

Due to the Karri-sized enormity of their family tree, Ella and Lucy where the kind of girls who followed the five-second-rule whenever their food dropped on the floor. There were no special lunch box orders lovingly packed in school backpacks, and no freshly laundered and perfectly ironed uniforms laid out for them each day. With no curfews imposed upon them, they were always first out and last in. Celeste had a curfew but her folks both worked a mixture of day and night shifts at the local parcel depot, which made her able to take advantage of their habit of losing track of all sense of time. Her other good friend, Macy, might be loose in the neighbourhood too, if her dad was away on his

FIFO stint up at Wheatstone. Macy had a two weeks on, two weeks off schedule that mirrored her father's roster at the oil and gas plant. She enjoyed a fortnight of crazy freedom when her mother was a single parent swimming with a snorkel on, followed by a fortnight of the Fort Knox treatment when her dad rolled in to hang up his high vis and brush the red dust off his boots.

There were others in their crowd too. Like Kingston. She'd known him since kindergarten, with his floppy dark hair that he was always pushing out of his eyes and that loud laugh that sometimes came out of nowhere. He'd kissed her last week at the back of the church during a game of truth or dare. She'd been his dare and had been all prepared for a peck, but he'd led her by the hand away from their friends and pressed her up against the wall while he made out with her properly, tongues and everything. It was a shame they were playing Ouija board spook games tonight in the spirit of Halloween and not truth or dare again.

With Pearl Jam still thundering, she levelled with the last house on the row of residential properties situated right next door to the church grounds. A figure at the front window caught her eye and made her jump. It was that gawking nerd. The one who sat in front of her in science class, with a curly mop of hair and a super fat head that was perfect to bounce her wooden ruler off. One time, a bunch of kids had filled his desk with empty sweet wrappers. When he found them, he turned around in class and stared right at her. His entire face had twisted into a contorted grimace, then his cheeks had blazed beetroot when she stuck her tongue out at him. He gave her the creeps, with his trousers that were too short and eyebrows that permanently met in the middle of his forehead. No wonder he spent most of his time frowning. Celeste might not live in a palace, but at least it wasn't as morbid as this dump, with its peeling blue front door and an overgrown garden with giant prickly bushes that lined the side of the carport all the way to where the green wheelie bin overflowed. Rumour around the school was that he was adopted. Made sense. Nobody around here made kids like him.

Celeste had asked him outright about it once. He'd denied it, but the pencil in his hand trembled for the whole of the rest of science class that day.

Celeste paused for a moment to stare at the peeking nerd. He raised both hands and started to wave, so she stuck two fingers up at him. It was fascinating, watching his arms flop to his sides. His head drooped along with them, as if a magnetic force of gravity was tugging everything to the ground. She sniggered as his glasses slipped from his nose and he disappeared, presumably to scramble around the floor to retrieve them.

She continued along, thankful it was finally getting dark as she reached the rusty gate at the entrance of the church grounds. It creaked as she pushed it open. Up ahead, Kingston and the twins sat in the graveyard, huddled around the Ouija board.

She wandered up and swiped her iPhone screen to knock off the music. 'No Macy yet?'

'Shhh,' said Ella. 'You'll disturb the spirits.'

'You didn't start without me, did you?' asked Celeste, sitting down on the brittle grass next to Kingston.

'No,' Ella and Lucy replied in unison.

Ella pulled her phone from her pocket. 'We were just getting psyched up. I'm waiting on a reply back from Jeremy.'

'Who?' Celeste asked.

'Jeremy. The chunk from science.'

'Why are you texting him?'

'We invited him along for some Halloween fun,' Kingston replied, making the twins laugh.

'I just walked past his house and saw him waving. He probably wanted to walk with me,' said Celeste. 'I don't get it, though. Since when do we hang out with losers?'

Ella's phone beeped and she checked her messages. 'That's him. He's on his way. We're not going to hang out with him, Celeste. We're going to hide. Hurry. Find a spot and wait for my signal. When it's time, jump out and give him the fright of his life.'

'What's the signal?' Celeste asked.

'You'll see.' Ella gave her a wicked grin.

They jumped to their feet and scrambled in different directions, leaving the Ouija board on the ground.

Celeste found a hollow in the trunk of an enormous tree, big enough to crouch inside. She could make out the silhouette of Jeremy cutting across the graveyard, his shoulders hunched. The sound of gravel crunching beneath his feet was suddenly overshadowed by a spine-chilling wailing noise.

Jeremy stopped in his tracks. 'Hello?'

The wailing continued, now accompanied by the loud fluttering and squawking noise of a colony of bats.

'Ella. Celeste. Are you here?' Jeremy's voice wavered.

Celeste grinned to herself as Ella cranked up the volume on whatever app or video clip she was using to create the spooky sound effects. A long, ghastly, howl pierced her eardrums and she knew the moment was now.

'Arrghhhhh,' she roared, emerging from her hiding place in the tree.

Ella, Lucy and Kingston shrieked along with her as they launched from their spots.

'The bogeyman is here!' Kingston charged full speed towards Jeremy.

Celeste ran towards the science nerd too. As she got closer to him, she noticed his body shaking, and his eyes seemed to be bulging almost out of his skull. She slowed down, but Jeremy was already staggering backwards. As he turned away, he tripped over a log and stumbled to the ground. They snorted with the hilarity of it all as he picked himself up and ran back towards the gate.

'Oh, that was priceless!' Lucy clapped.

'He looked terrified,' said Celeste. 'Maybe we took it a bit too far.'

'No way. Best Halloween moment ever,' said Ella.

Kingston wandered back over to the Ouija board and sat down to form a ring around it with Ella and Lucy. Celeste squeezed in next to him.

'Where did you find such sick noises?' Celeste asked Ella.

'YouTube.'

They relaxed in their circle, unpicking every second of their prank with Jeremy, replaying the scene over and over until Celeste felt an uneasy heaviness develop in the pit of her stomach.

'I wish we'd caught footage of it. Something like that would get a million YouTube views,' said Lucy. 'Ella was right. It really was the best Halloween moment ever.'

'Halloween isn't over yet. Let's play.' Kingston glanced at Celeste. 'And no cheating.'

'Never.' Celeste blushed as she placed her finger gently over his on the planchette.

Kingston cleared his throat and raised his eyes to the heavens. 'Will anyone die this Halloween?'

Celeste held her breath and then felt the tremor as the planchette began to move slowly towards the letter J.

It picked up speed, faster and faster, pointing and spinning.

Kingston called out each letter, his voice booming in the stillness of the night. 'J E R E M Y.'

The planchette stopped.

A look of confusion passed between the twins and Kingston, but Celeste felt sick. She knew what it meant. Jeremy had spoken, delivering a message to them all from a dark place filled with bullies, depression, and gun violence. One riddled with consequences.

'Maybe we should go and check if the science nerd is okay?' suggested Celeste.

'Mmmwwahaha.' Kingston let rip his maniacal laugh. 'You're kidding, right?'

Celeste shrugged. 'We should cut him a break.'

'Why?' asked Lucy.

'He's a weirdo,' said Ella.

'It's Halloween. The more of us the better. We can easily ask him to come back. He'll be perfect for playing the Ouija board with.' Celeste got up and brushed the grass of her jeans. 'I'm going to get him.'

There was an eerie silence as she headed back through the cemetery, so she popped her headphones back in and pressed replay on the Pearl Jam track. It took her a couple of minutes to reach the rusty gate. She gave it a shove and turned into the street.

A blue strobe caught her attention, a blur in the distance. It took only a few moments for it to come into focus. A police car was hurtling uphill towards her. She paused in her steps as it swerved in towards the curb and halted outside the science nerd's house. Another vehicle followed, an ambulance with its lights also flashing.

The sound of their sirens was masked by her music.

Jeremy.

Jeremy.

Jeremy.

She opened her mouth to scream his name but all that came out was a deathly silence.

Silver Lining

The silver helium balloon has been shrivelling over the last few days. It was hand-delivered, tied to a beautiful bouquet of bright yellow sunflowers – the only flowers I've received lately that weren't weaved into a wreath. So thoughtful of my sister to send them a few weeks after Mark's funeral. She's an angel. Added a note that the sun will eventually shine in my life once again. The kindness from everyone else has faded, much like the musky smell of Mark on the pillow of our bed. No more casseroles left on my front step. People have their own problems to deal with. Not that I'm seeking ongoing sympathy but becoming a widow in my twenties was so unexpected.

I pull my blonde hair into a ponytail. It feels greasy. Can't recall the last time I washed it. Tug on a tracksuit and my ancient runners, then force myself to venture outside to pick up a few essential groceries. When I get to the mall, I'm drawn to a gift shop selling candles and condolences cards. End up buying another silver helium balloon. When I get home, I'm unable to stop crying as I stare at it. After a while, I get up and fetch a carving knife from the wooden block in the kitchen. Think about using it to slice into my wrists. Checking out would be the easiest way to run away from my problems. Instead, I poke a tiny hole in the neck of the balloon and put my mouth over it. I suck the air out, hoping to become light enough to float up to heaven to see Mark. Instead, I become light-headed. A laugh escapes my lips, high-pitched and uncontrollable. It snowballs into a bout of hysteria ricocheting around the walls of my apartment. So glad the helium balloon has a silver lining.

Adrenalin Junkie

Hayden's heart raced as Carmen walked in the room. His hands shook as he gulped down a cup of ice-cold water, which did nothing to moisten his dry mouth. She looked stunning, dressed in a trouser suit that perfectly accentuated her curves. The navy fabric complemented her blue eyes, which were staring at him now with a piercing intensity he'd never experienced with any other woman in the past. He liked the elegant gold studs in her ears and the strands of blonde hair that escaped her bun and curled around her heart-shaped face. He ran his fingers through his own dark hair to smooth down any loose ends. Hopefully, she was just as observant as he was and noticed the trouble he'd gone to with his appearance. Taking the time to shave down to a baby-smooth chin was a concession he made only for her.

'Thank goodness we were lucky enough to get a table without a reservation,' Hayden said as she crossed the room that was packed with diners. 'This place has gourmet food to die for. Even the sausage and mash has Michelin stars.'

A flicker of a smile crossed her face. She wasn't one for letting her emotions show, which made the challenge of breaking down her barriers just that bit more interesting. She was always so poised, as if downplaying her incredible looks to avoid unwanted attention. Her sculptured cheeks were always devoid of make-up and there was never any hint of cleavage showing. It was unusual to meet such a beautiful woman who downplayed her looks the way she did. He wished he was alone with her now, ripping off her underwear and touching her wherever he wanted. It was torture sitting here with his lust building up. They hadn't consummated their relationship yet, but he knew it would be explosive when they did.

He thought back to the last time he'd been so infatuated by a woman. Brook Robinson had been something special and their time together one wild adventure. Vivid memories flowed, like it was only yesterday and not three years ago that he had met her.

*

She sucker-punched him from afar when he spotted her amidst the crowd at Hillary's Harbour on a blistering hot Saturday afternoon. The heel of her strappy white shoe had caught between the slats of the wooden boardwalk that sat on stilts above the water, connecting the restaurants, bars, and craft shops. The sudden jerk made her coffee fall and brown liquid splashed on the leather of her footwear.

Hayden crossed the few metres from where he'd been nursing a cold beer while he enjoyed passing the time people watching. 'You okay?'

'Brings a new meaning to skinny flat white when you don't get a single sip of calories.'

Hayden laughed, enjoying her humour and the strong lilt of her British accent, which he couldn't quite narrow down to a specific part of the UK. 'Can I buy you another?'

'Not sure I can move.' The woman gave her foot a wiggle, but her shoe was well and truly wedged in the gap.

'Take off the shoe. Maybe I can get it out in one piece.'

Hayden watched her long fingers unhook the buckle of her strap and the most perfect bare foot slip from the shoe. Her toenails were painted a pale shade of lilac with a tiny daisy on each of them. They were a masterpiece, better than anything he'd seen hanging in the local art galleries of Western Australia. He could barely stop staring at them as he knelt to ease the shoe free.

He handed it back to her. 'There you go.'

'Thanks. I'm Brook by the way.'

'Hayden.'

Electricity sizzled as they shook hands and he instantly knew from the stirring in his loins that she was the one. Blondes always attracted him, but this one was something else. Her long wavy locks looked soft and natural in colour, not the harsh peroxide blonde hair that was so brittle you could start a bushfire if you lit a match within a kilometre radius of it. She had a willowy figure shown off to perfection in denim shorts, and the gypsy multicoloured top with enormous sleeves made him think she might be the kind of carefree spirit he loved. And that pout. It was coy and sexy, with perfect pink lips that just begged to be kissed.

Hayden bought her a fresh, overpriced coffee in a trendy establishment with decadent furnishings and the best ocean views. It was a small price to pay to hear her life story.

Brook told him she was born in the north of England, in Newcastle-upon-Tyne, which put him out of his misery trying to second guess the origin of her accent. She was a working-class Geordie who had done well enough in her education to claw her way out of a crime-riddled government housing estate. Qualifying as a nurse had provided her with a golden ticket into Australia.

'Which hospital are you working at?' he asked when she'd finished talking about her background.

'None yet. I only arrived two weeks ago, so I've just been checking out Perth city since then. I've a new job lined up in Mandurah, though, starting next month, so I'll be moving down there.'

'So you don't know anyone?'

'I know you.'

Hayden grinned. His life in comparison was ordinary. Since leaving school, he'd worked in the same deadbeat job as a debt collector for the government, chasing overpayments from people on benefits who couldn't afford to put food on the table. The depressing work was enough to drive a man to insanity. He tried to offset this mundane existence by spending his downtime appreciating untrodden territory where nobody but diehard hikers like him would think to explore. He quickly established Brook loved the outdoors too.

As they chatted, several boats cruised in and out of their pens, expensive toys paid for by Western Australia's mining boom, then the huge commercial ferry pulled in. Hundreds of tourists offloaded their luggage and bicycles after a weekend on Rottnest Island, the spectacular playground forty-five minutes offshore from where they were sitting. Its outline was visible across the turquoise ocean, a magnet attracting the next wave of visitors to enjoy some relaxation time there.

'I'm beefing up my fitness training for this week-long Cape to Cape walk that's coming up soon.' He watched her remove the plastic lid from her coffee to blow on it. 'It goes from Cape Naturaliste Lighthouse to Cape Leeuwin Lighthouse. Trekking and cycling around Rottnest would be perfect as part of my exercise ramp-up. I don't suppose you have a bike?'

'One of the first things I bought when I got here.'

'See, I knew as soon as I met you we'd have so much in common. You up for a day trip?' Hayden beamed, glad that he'd worn his favourite sports T-shirt and khaki shorts. He guessed she was in her twenties, certainly younger than him by a few years, but he regularly pumped up a sweat at the gym to keep in decent shape.

'When?'

'How about tomorrow? I've got a couple of things to do first thing over there on the island, but we can meet around eleven outside the main bakery if you get the mid-morning ferry. There's only one bakery and it's close to the main jetty where you get off. It would be cool to hang out again.'

'Let's do it. Give me your mobile number in case anything changes, otherwise I'll see you there.'

They swapped numbers, and he told her about the ticket booth at the marina entrance where she could book the ferry. Reluctantly, he said goodbye and watched her stroll off. He could have talked to her for hours, and it seemed an impossible task to have to wait a whole day before he saw her again.

*

The early morning ferry was busy as it made the crossing from Hillary's Harbour. He took a seat next to an Australian family with an excited toddler in a Batman T-shirt. The boy kept moving from his father's knee to his mother's as if playing musical chairs. Hayden couldn't wait to get away from them and onto the sanctuary of the island and was pleased the ferry pulled into the jetty at Thomson Bay bang on time. A delay would have been unbearable but thankfully rush hour congestion was not a problem that the Indian Ocean suffered from.

Hayden had purposely departed on the ferry before Brook to have time to steady his nerves before she got there. First date butterflies were something he'd never been able to manage well. His confidence in approaching Brook was smoke and mirrors. He'd spent years fumbling through awkward interactions with the opposite sex.

After his black mountain bike was offloaded from the ferry, he slung on his backpack and cycled into the main square in the settlement centre, nestled amidst low-rise self-catering accommodation. He set his front wheel in the metal bike rack, pleased at the peace and quiet that was a result of cars being prohibited on Rottnest. The only methods of travel around the island were on foot, bike, or on the circular shuttle bus.

He grabbed a takeaway coffee from one of the restaurants and settled down on an empty bench to take in his surroundings. The Rottnest Island Authority had done a good job of preventing too much commercialisation, with not much more than a grocery store, an ice creamery that sold every weird flavour under the sun, and the large bakery. Sympathetic development of an A-class reserve, done to protect the island's nineteen square kilometres of natural beauty. A group of furry quokkas meandered around on a large patch of grass next to him. One wandered too close and he hissed it away. Tourists seemed to love the native marsupials that carried their young in a pouch like kangaroos, but to him they were no better than flea-infested, oversized rats. Long ago, he'd realised some quokka were skittish and wild, while others seemed to relish human company. He preferred to enjoy nature that was more predictable than animals. Smart trees that never failed to adapt to the seasons and shed their dead leaves in the breeze, the treacherous rips that were invisible to the naked eye but were guaranteed to be present under the ocean surface, or the phenomenal sunsets that left their burnt-orange trail across the sky, night after night on the western side of Australia.

He finished the last of his coffee and tossed the cardboard cup in the bin next to where he sat. Spreading his arms along the back of the bench, he leaned back to watch families, couples, and individuals like him gradually fill the square, until eventually the area was a swarming beehive. The tranquillity of the museum beckoned to him, so he wandered over to the original limestone building housed inside the old mill and hay store. The main wooden door was propped open, so he stepped inside.

'Morning.' An elderly lady with cropped grey hair and kindly eyes greeted him. 'It's a gold coin donation if you would like to look around. This place has such marvellous history. It was built by Aboriginal prisoners in 1857.'

Hayden didn't care too much about hearing stories of criminals who wound up caged behind bars, but he rummaged in his backpack and pulled a dollar from his wallet. 'I'll definitely take you up on that.'

'Are you alone?'

'Sure am. I'm just over for a day of cycling and thought I'd check this place out before I get started.'

'Let me show you around. It won't take long. You're the first one here.'

Hayden relaxed as they wandered around. He was given a history lesson as they checked out artefacts housed in glass cases and exhibitions of photographs and information displayed around the walls. He didn't want to hurt the curator's feelings by telling her he already knew all about the old prison, indigenous inhabitants and shipwrecks. There had been numerous family holidays spent here as a kid, before his father ran off with another woman and left him with a depressed mother who depended on her only son to change every plug in the house. He knew every inch of the island better than he knew the corners of his own soul.

When his tour was finished, Hayden thanked the lady and headed back to the main square. As he walked there, he spotted that the next ferry had moored at the jetty and people were busy disembarking as their bikes were offloaded by the crew.

His phone beeped with a text from Brook: *I'm here.*

He wiped the message and sat on another bench outside the bakery and waited. Moments later, she caught his eye, waving frantically with one arm as she steered her red bike towards him with the other. He remained seated, rooted to the spot as he drank her in. Her glorious long, golden hair was loose today, popping out beneath her helmet to grace her shoulders.

'Hey.' The smile she gave him was enormous.

'You look amazing.'

'In Lycra shorts?'

'Trust me, you look good. Shall we get straight to it before it gets too hot? It's going to be another summer scorcher today.'

Brook nodded.

'There's a fantastic swimming spot up past Geordie Bay. We'll head that way first.'

'Geordie Bay. That's an ironic place to visit for a Geordie like me.' She chuckled as they fell into formation, him up front, her tailing him.

There were so many beautiful routes to take around Rottnest, but he chose the remote track that took them out of the settlement, through woodland and up past Hershal Lake.

'Wait,' Brook called from behind him after they'd cycled a few kilometres.

He stopped and turned as she climbed off her bike after coming to a halt on the shore of the lake. Piles of natural salt gathered at the water's edge beside her feet.

'This is breathtaking.'

A huge bird glided past them.

'Check that out,' said Hayden, getting off his own bike and walking to her side. 'It's an osprey eagle.'

'I've never seen anything like it.'

Hayden pulled out his phone and breathed in her heady scent as he leaned in next to her to take a selfie. She smelt of clean laundry, as if she'd dipped herself in an excessive amount of fabric softener.

'These salt lakes are a Rottnest phenomenon. The island is small but there are several more lakes like this one.'

'You'll have to send that snap to me.'

'Later. There's no phone signal here.'

'I never dreamed this place would be such a wildlife haven.'

'Wait until you see more of it. Every beach is unique and has a different name. The Basin and Little Salmon Bay both have mind-blowing snorkelling, but they get packed in summer. I prefer the quieter coves.'

'Let's go then. The faster we cycle, the more we get to see before the ferry sails back tonight.'

Hayden couldn't wipe the grin off his face. Her enthusiasm was infectious, and he couldn't wait to get to the spot that was his favourite place in the whole world.

*

They left their bikes on the ground behind a tall, prickly bush and weaved through the fauna, clapping their hands as they went to send any snakes into hiding. The view was stunning as they rambled through bushland, curving around a cliff overlooking glinting ocean. They clambered over a steep section to find a lagoon nestled behind it, enclosed on all sides with jagged rocks.

When they reached the edge of the lagoon, they dropped their backpacks onto a small patch of pristine sand.

'Unbelievable!' Brook lifted her long hair and twisted it into a ponytail secured with an elastic band from her wrist.

Hayden noticed the dampness around her neckline. 'We should

swim to cool off.' He pulled off his T-shirt and watched as Brook followed suit and peeled off her vest.

Her cerise and white polka dot bikini top was strapless, but she had fresh tan marks where her vest straps had been, a sign of foreign skin still adapting to the wicked Australian rays.

He bent to rummage in his backpack and pulled out rubber reef shoes, black neoprene gloves and his diving knife, which he strapped to his thigh over one leg of his shorts.

'Wow, you came prepared.'

He nodded towards the ocean. 'This is Australia. There are all kinds of predators out there. When you get into the water, stick close and follow where I stand. There's long seagrass underwater and some sharp rocks that can scratch your feet. If we can get to the far side, there's a submerged cave with a tiny tunnel leading from the lagoon to the ocean. If you're up for the challenge, it's pretty cool to swim through.'

'My middle name is adrenalin junkie.'

'I'll wait for you on that flattish rock over there. It's right beside the cave.'

Brook nodded, and Hayden gave her one last smile before lowering himself into the water. It was cold at first, but the sharp needles were refreshing, putting him on high alert for the adventure ahead. The water only reached his waist, but as he waded out, it became deep enough to swim across.

His middle name was adrenalin junkie too. A rush was pumping through his veins by the time he clambered onto the flat rock on the other side, because he knew he'd finally found the perfect girl to share this experience with.

*

Hayden shook his head to get the image of Brook out of his head. The ending had been abrupt, but even though it had been three years since she'd gone from his life forever, he still replayed every moment of his relationship with her every day. It was over with Brook and it was driving him insane thinking about her all the time. He knew the only remedy was to find another woman to replace her. It was about Carmen now. She was the lucky one.

Carmen caught his eye again and the stare lingered longer than necessary before she averted her eyes. She fiddled with a jacket button on her navy uniform and he guessed he was getting under her skin. That was how relationship was meant to be: two people so in tune with the moment they could read exactly what was going on inside the other's mind. He wanted her and, from the way she watched him so intently, he suspected that she knew it.

He looked down bashfully and placed his hands over his groin under the table. Any obvious desire visible through his pants would make her jumpy, not because she'd experienced it yet, but because she knew exactly what he was incarcerated for. It took a lot of patience to chip away at her defences. Based on his history, it would be understandable for Carmen to be afraid of their relationship becoming physical. For three years now, he'd been working on gaining her trust by behaving impeccably in her presence. His reward for acting with demure restraint was usually an extra minute of yard exercise time or throwing him a rare smile in the corridor, but it was slow progress. Eventually, he was sure she would slip up on her endeavours to avoid being alone with him.

Grabbing her was the monumental event he was waiting patiently for. He was still an adrenalin junkie, only these days the rush that he craved was fuelled by narcotics. Amphetamines, benzos or whatever he could get his hands on. The drugs would heighten the thrill he'd have when that window of opportunity came with Carmen. It would be all-consuming, frantic, and there would be no coming back from it.

It would make his time with Brook pale in comparison. With her, he'd enjoyed several leisurely hours in one of the world's most incredible secluded locations, turning every fantasy he'd ever had into reality, before he finally slit her throat with his dive knife. With all his careful planning, he'd nearly gotten away with it too. He'd indulged in a handful of crazy trysts before, but nothing where he tipped things right over the delicate line between life and death. For so long, he'd been strong in resisting the urge to take his desires to another level, but Brook was his weakness. He'd intentionally chosen her as the one to satisfy his needs because she was a new arrival to the country; someone nobody would miss straight away.

Meticulous details had been thought through. Making sure they travelled to Rottnest Island on different ferries. Ensuring he'd been seen by the Aussie family with the Batman brat. The curator had been another witness of his solitary visit to the museum; just another tourist enjoying the island. He'd doubled back to sink Brook's bike too, before he cycled back to Thomson Bay for the last ferry home.

It was that stupid 'I'm here' text she'd sent him when she first got off the ferry that directed police attention onto him. He'd filled her bag with rocks before tossing it into the ocean and thought her phone had been in it, but it hadn't. It was found in the sand next to where they had stripped down to their swimwear. That message led investigators to him and they'd found the photo on his own phone of them by the lake. Before he was caught, he'd gone to delete that selfie so many times, but could never manage to trash it. Just looking at her face had excited him, over and over again. So exuberant. So trusting.

His biggest misjudgement of all, though, had been thinking the ocean would pull her body far out to sea after he pushed her over the lagoon edge into the waves. Instead, it washed up on Geordie Bay five days after he killed her. He cursed the great whites for not being around when he needed them most. He knew sharks were unpredictable and hadn't solely relied on their hunger, but his miscalculation of the riptide had cost him dearly.

With Carmen, their time together would be short. At best, he would only be able to grab a few intense minutes with her behind the silver shelving in the laundry room, or in the food storage cupboard just off the main kitchen, before an avalanche of her prison officer colleagues descended upon them with their batons and cuffs. He would need to be quick when he screwed the screw. Still, it would be long enough to see the rollercoaster of emotions that would pass over her face. The anger he hoped Carmen would feel when she realised she'd finally been cornered, then resignation when he had his way with her. What a kick to reverse the power she asserted over him every day when she locked him in his cell after communal mealtimes like this or put him through an impromptu strip search. She was a nosy bitch, always entering his personal space to look for contraband. He would put his mouth over her nose so she could smell his breath. Maybe he'd even bite her nostrils. He would relish the build-up of her discomfort and get off on making her scream. With pain or with pleasure, it was all the same.

Finally, before he was hauled off to the slot, he would wrap his hands around her neck and squeeze. He would enjoy watching her gasp for breath before sadness etched itself forever on her beautiful face. And he wouldn't blink in those final predictable few seconds as the light in her eyes went out.

He tore a chunk from his bread roll to mop up the mash in the durable, split-resistant compartment tray. Carmen's stare returned and he bowed his head demurely, holding back from running his tongue over his lips. It had been euphoric with Brook, and it would be even better with this one.

The adventure worth getting a life sentence for.

Cream

Ice cream melts on the ground, sticky caramel sauce seeping between the cracks. A young girl in pigtails cries. Her dad scoops her up in his arms and carries her into the natural pool carved into the rocks along the shore. She squeals again, this time in delight as they hit the chill of the water. I love how a bad situation can be turned around with those reliable hands of his.

Suncream drips down another man's bronzed back. A woman's hands rub it in, leisurely, massaging his broad shoulders, down his arms. Her fingers disappear down the waist band of his boardies. When she's done, making sure the cream is spread evenly and is fully absorbed, he turns and faces her. Sunnies cover his eyes. She pushes them up and his blue eyes stare at her face. He smiles before he kisses her.

Skin. Mine is cream without a single freckle. I burn too easily to let the sun bake me red raw. Even though there are no walls and people surround me in the waves and along the beach, under the umbrella I have solitude. It's invaluable time for self-absorption, alone here in the shade. No lunch boxes to pack for my child. No shirts to iron for my husband. No insatiable lover to satisfy.

A gust of wind blows sand onto my body. Grainy and uncomfortable, it clings to my bare legs. I brush it off. Wish I could brush off the mess I am in just as easily.

My husband comes towards me, water dripping down his familiar body. The love of my life since high school. Our thirteenth wedding anniversary is next week. Lace is the official gift. I've bought an absurdly expensive black bra and matching pants. Feel hot in them.

'I dropped my ice cream, Mummy,' my beautiful little girl says, plonking down her wet bottom on the corner of my striped towel.

‘But we had fun anyway, sweetheart, didn’t we?’ her dad says.

‘Yes, Daddy.’

From the corner of my eye, I see the other man. Blue eyes. Rubbing cream into her back now. Last night it was my body his hands roamed over. I’ll see him tomorrow. He’ll go crazy for the new underwear.

Cream sunhat. Big brim.

I pull it down to block out the view. Inside, my mind lets out an anguished SCREAM.

The Seven-year Itch

The itch is worse than getting a nettle sting while trampling the overgrown hill at the back of the estate. Fingers frantically scratch at the scalp, trying to get temporary relief.

'Stop it.' My sister, Mary, swipes my hand away so she can keep picking through my hair.

Lukewarm water splashes around us. We've been in the bath so long I've developed wrinkled fingertips. Mary puts another dollop of conditioner on my hair and combs it through.

'Can you see any?' I ask.

'I'm looking. Keep still.'

We've both had nits for weeks. My straight auburn hair shows them up easier than her dark curly hair. Different dads. Mary is ten now, so she can't even remember anything about her dad. He left when she was a toddler. I'm two years younger and my dad only left last year. He moved out to make space for Danny, the shopkeeper from the corner grocery store. Danny's clothes stink of aftershave. Dad always smelled nice, of laundry powder. I miss him.

'Got one,' Mary says, dragging her nails down my long hair.

'Show me.' I swivel my head to look at Mary, who is sitting behind me in the bath. A nit is squashed between her finger and thumb. 'Yuk. They're gross. I hate them.'

'Will you do mine now, Sammy?' Mary asks.

The water sloshes as we turn around so she can sit between my legs. I begin searching. I find a couple of small ones, babies. There must still be eggs hatching somewhere in her mop. By the time I'm finished, the water is freezing and we climb out, wrapping ourselves in thin towels that are as rough as sandpaper.

'Race you.' Mary gets a head start as she darts from the bathroom.

She's already in front of the small electric fire when I get to the living room.

'Move over,' I say.

She shuffles along and we snuggle up, still in our wet towels. When I've stopped shivering, I head along the passage to our bedroom and grab our matching red and white striped nighties from under our pillows on the bunkbeds. I have to climb the ladder to get my sister's. She gets the top bunk because she's older.

We tug them on in front of the fire, laughing at the wonky bottom of mine. Mum bought me the same size as Mary because they were in the sale and they only had that one bigger size left. She cut the hem off with scissors so I would stop tripping over it, but now it's all ragged with loose threads unravelling everywhere.

'What time do you think they'll be back?' I ask Mary.

'Late, probably. Shall we watch *Top of the Pops* and then we can talk in bed?'

I nod. It's Friday night and Mum always goes out to watch rock bands play at the Working Men's Club down the town with Danny. It's my favourite night of the week because she leaves us a big packet of cheese and onion crisps to share with a pile of cheese sandwiches cut into squares. Anything cheese flavour is yum. We also get to watch whatever we want on the new black and white TV.

Mary pulls the cling film off the plate of sandwiches. I put a handful of crisps between my white bread and shove it in my mouth, crunching away.

'That's disgusting.' Mary picks at her crisps gingerly with two fingers.

We both giggle again. Duran Duran comes on *Top of the Pops* and we dance around the living room to 'The Reflex'. I do a handstand against the wall, my nightie falling over my damp hair, flashing my pants. I can hold a handstand for almost a whole song, but Mary is much better. She can stay upside down until her face turns so red I worry she has no blood left in her feet. When I'm older, I'll probably be just as good at handstands as her. Maybe I'll get the top bunk too one day.

*

The torch shakes in my hand. Under the tent of my quilt, *The Magic Faraway Tree* has just stopped at the Land of Slaps. I read the chapter as fast as I can, trying to get to the next place before I fall asleep. Hopefully it's the Land of Goodies or Presents. Somewhere nice to escape to instead of a bad land. I shudder as I read about Moonface and Silky getting hurt. Dame Slap is the meanest person I've ever read about. Downstairs, I can hear fighting. Something smashed after Mum and Danny came in from the pub and they've not stopped screaming at each other since.

'You awake?' Mary whispers.

'Yes.'

'Do you think we should go downstairs and tell them to stop?'

'Dunno.'

I close my book and stick my turtle head out from under the shell of my bedding so I can listen better. Danny is accusing Mum of staring at someone else in the pub.

'Do you think it's true and Mum did look at another man?' Mary asks.

'Dunno.'

'You don't know anything.'

My sister is right. I don't know anything about what is going on. Maybe Mum did stare at someone else. Perhaps we will get another new dad soon. If we do, I hope he's nicer than Danny.

'I'll go downstairs if you do.'

Mary is silent so I stay where I am. There's no way I'm getting out of bed without her.

Downstairs, the row is getting worse. Two big bangs make me jump, like furniture is being moved, then suddenly it's replaced by Mum making strange grunting sounds.

'What is that?' Mary whispers.

'Dunno.' I bite my lip to try and stop myself from crying, but the tears are already out.

'I think we should get up and go and help her.'

'Okay.' I wipe my eyes and nose on the corner of my pillowcase and climb out of bed, but then Mum suddenly cries out and the grunting stops.

'Get back in,' Mary whispers urgently. 'I think they're coming.'

I leap back into the bottom bunk as the noise of footsteps climbing the stairs gets louder. My torch is still on, so I knock off the power button and hide the book and torch under my damp pillow. I tug the bedding up to my chin and screw my eyes tightly closed in case Mum comes in to check on us. Even though I'm frightened, I hope in my heart that she does stick her head in the door to whisper goodnight. Just this once.

She doesn't.

*

The itch to leave Newcastle-upon-Tyne is so intense I could scratch it until I bleed. Mary is long gone, living in student nursing home digs on the other side of the River Tyne. She'll make a kind nurse. I get a lump in my throat when I think about the way she took care of me when we were growing up. Sometimes she stood in between my head and Danny's palm. Only a pretty special big sister would do that.

Mum will be mad when I leave. She needs the money from my Saturday job at the bakery to pay for the rent and her Friday nights out drinking rum and black. When she realises I've been stashing portions of my wage in the plant pot at the back of the garden shed, all hell will break loose. Exams are over now at school and I plan to put a decent chunk of map between us as quickly as I can. Don't care where I end up, as long as it's out of arm's reach. Don't know how I managed to get such good results with all the distractions at school. Wasn't easy navigating around the truanting and taunting crowd. I hate the mean girls almost as much as I hate Mum and Danny. Don't know what good a bunch of straight-A grades will do, especially since Mum never once looked at my school report, but I know there is something better than this out there waiting for me.

*

The itch to go home is unbearable. It will be fun to fly back to the hustle and bustle of England and compare my minimalist flat in East Perth to the mess of my old bedroom in the north-east. Excitement builds at the thought of smelling the old copies of *Malory Towers* on the bookshelf above my rickety single bed. The practicalities of my Kindle cannot possibly outweigh an entire paperback museum of Enid Blyton works.

My mouth waters at the thought of eating Mum's best home-cooked culinary delight of corned beef hash. When I was a kid, she used to mash the potato with a tin of marrowfat peas. Not seen that anywhere on the menu of the gastro venues overlooking the Swan River.

One side of my Louis Vuitton case is packed with gifts. Beautifully wrapped with paper covered in the brightest wild flowers. They are tied with a sparkling white ribbon. Admittedly, I overindulged on the shopping spree for unusual handmade goods of real leather and soft silk. Pretty stuff Mum will drool over. It's been years since I left home, long enough for her to forgive me for running away. She never chased me after I got a one-way ticket outta there. Moving from Newcastle to London was the best thing I ever did. Love being independent. The phone calls I place to her have been tense ever since, but when she sees I've bought her new fella, Martin, cufflinks, it should blow away the cobwebs so we can start over. I've no idea if Danny left Mum or she traded up to a better option sourced from the Working Men's Club, but good riddance to bad rubbish.

I tap her number into my smart device and hold my breath while it rings.

She answers, 'Hello,' with that familiar high-pitched lilt in her voice.

'It's me, Sammy.'

The lengthy silence is broken by the sound of a cruise liner passing by the window of my digs. Wish Mum could see the view I have over the water. I've lost count how many times I've seen dolphins and beautiful black swans. Transferring from London to Western Australia with the company I work for was a dream come true.

'I was thinking of coming home for a few days,' I say.

'Why would you do that?'

'It's been a long time. I'm due a visit.'

'Nothing's changed.'

'That's perfect, Mum. I can sleep in my old room.'

'Oh, that's changed. Brian uses it as a gym.'

'Brian. I thought his name was Martin?'

'Oh, don't start.'

'I wasn't starting anything. I'm sure he's lovely.'

'When were you thinking of coming?'

'This week. I've bought my ticket and I'm all packed. I don't mind sleeping on the sofa for a night or two.'

'Please yourself. As long as you pay rent while you're here. You know how expensive groceries are.'

Words tumble around in my head, jostling for the right ones to make their way to my vocal cords. The phone quivers in my hand.

'I've got to go, Mum.'

'Wait! So, are you definitely coming home or not?'

'Not.'

I swipe the glass screen to disconnect and collapse into the armchair in my lounge that has been upholstered in an exquisite fabric covered in birds. My wings were once clipped, but now I'm free to fly wherever I choose. Perhaps sometime soon I will migrate to a new part of the world to explore new cultures, meet different people and discover hidden opportunities.

There are two paths I can take. The one that allows me to accept the things I cannot change and embrace the future. Or the other, where I take the road home again, where the path back into the past is way less travelled than it should be for a girl who hasn't seen her mum for seven years.

The itch to unpack my suitcase is overwhelming.

Fearless Girl

Monday morning can't get any worse. Coffee spills on white silk blouse. Miss the Melbourne city bus and wait ages for a cab. Boss points out my tardiness in front of the entire team. He's got it in for me. I'm the only one not modelling pinstripe pants and a paisley tie.

'Serves us right for hiring the token gesture to diversity,' he smirks.

Go for a walk at lunchtime to cool off. New statue has arrived on Federation Square. *Fearless Girl.* Made her debut on Wall Street. Buy a double espresso and head back

You got this, girl.

You got this!

Monologue of a Sardine

My breath exhales in a visible fog as I sit in my living room nursing a cup of coffee. The warm drink is a futile attempt to combat the cold chill creeping through the cracks around my ancient windows. The television screen is beaming out images of a mother who abandoned her two children and has now been reunited with them. Daytime TV sucks, but I can't bring myself to turn it off.

Every time I watch a show, my fingers sink into my hair, twisting and pulling the strands, wondering if some of the premature greying is a side effect of the things I see before my very eyes. Blinking is unwanted; I'm drawn in by the sheer stupidity of the human race. The way we can divide our personalities between extreme love one moment and intense hatred the next. How most of us work our fingers to the bone and have nothing to show for it, except a crummy piece of real estate rented from the government, with mould on the ceiling and drug addicts squatting in the stairwell. The audacity of the millennials who bunk off school and still somehow land a job paying a six-figure salary with a company car and a lucrative pension. We are a bizarre species, to be sure.

When I tune into the news, the headline stories hit me hardest. I'm quite sure I'm not the only viewer appalled to listen to how one brother has killed another with his bare fists. I'm afraid for civilisation with so many incidents of religious fundamentalists blowing up communities in the Middle East. It's incomprehensible to think someone might be so extreme in their views that they self-destruct themselves and everyone around them like that.

The pretty blonde news anchor, who always wears the brightest coloured jackets like she's a pack of Smarties (orange today – third time she's worn it), pouts as she shares sickening snippets about a primary school teacher with six bodies buried in his garden.

We are all born to die, but I hope to go in my sleep, with nothing more than a loud snore to upset the peace. There seems such an imbalance of the fairness scales in the way some people receive the privilege of more dignity in their departure than others. It can only be serendipity. I'm not delusional in thinking there is any logic to this madness when we are a nation of sardines crammed in a claustrophobic tin. The unfairness stinks from those bad fish who float in the contaminated brine well past their sell-by date.

It's a miracle I don't go mad myself, when so much of my time is spent dwelling on these horrendously depressing facts of life. This deep perspective I have on humanity is a curse; a sixth sense for tragedy and morbid death obsession that I feed with an insatiable appetite for the noir entertainment of the news. Since being an awkward freckled primary school outcast, with holes in my socks and greasy pigtails in my hair, my life became overshadowed by death; animals with their final breath ripped from them at the cruel hand of Mother. A chicken, thrashing as the kitchen knife sliced its head off, then feathers still as blood spilled to the ground. My goldfish dead in the lavatory, flushed away as punishment because I accidentally left the laundry hanging on the line during a rainstorm when I was eight. And when I was twelve, Mother told me my dog, Archie, had been lethally poisoned by sewerage water, even though his tail wagged like crazy when I played fetch with him that very morning. It upset me no end, made worse because there was nobody to talk to about it. Father was long gone by then, off with another woman who didn't give a damn.

In hindsight, I can't blame Father. Well, not entirely. Mother dished out so much misery it's a wonder he didn't top himself. She's a mongrel breed. A nasty fishwife, with the sleek body of a panther, claws of a tiger and the tongue of a serpent.

'Get off your fat arse and get to work,' she would scream, even though Father worked holes in his boots down at the building site and always handed his wage packet over to her at the end of the week. 'Are you a man or a sodding mouse?' She would hiss all the names under the sun, slapping him around the head and laughing at his manhood.

It wasn't much better for me. While I was too young to send out to work to contribute with paying the rent, she made me pay tenfold for the mistakes I made instead.

The day I got home from high school too late to make the dinner was one of the worst.

'You good for nothing dirt bag. Look at you, wandering in when you feel like it. Do you think this place is a goddamn hotel?' She grasped a clump of my auburn curls in her hand.

My scalp hurt so much it was impossible to explain the teacher kept me behind to tell me my essay about saving the planet was one of the best she'd read in a long time.

'What do you think these ears are for, you stupid cow?'

Strands of my hair were pulled out, and if that wasn't enough, she yanked my earlobe so hard it dislodged any wax I might have accumulated there and left me with a headache for a week. I took small solace in being able to hold back the tears, even when the belt came off her jeans.

I miss Father every day, but Mother can go to hell.

When the men started coming, I kept my head down and tried to stay out of their way. Most of them were okay. In the gate, through to Mother's bedroom, door closed for half an hour, then off they went with a swagger in their step. To drown out the grunting, I used to pump up the volume on the remote. It was a lot easier to tune into the news channel and I'm ashamed to say I found rotten comfort in knowing worse situations were going on in the world than mine.

But one or two of the customers were bastards. Twice I ended up with a black and blue eye for looking at them as they cut through the house to Mother's lair. Other times, I didn't look at all, but felt a stare burning a hole the back of my head as their eyes undressed me. I got off lightly, though. Even though Mother was once held down by two of them in front of me, I was never raped. She told me afterwards she had no problem being humiliated like that, but her bulging eyes as it happened told me a different story.

'Give 'em what they want and they'll come back begging,' she said.

Well, Mother can shove her thesis to the bottom of her leopard-print handbag. I'll never let a man lay a finger on me as long as I live. Some people turn out exactly like their folks. Me, I'll do anything to avoid turning into Mother.

I left school with top grades and a better than average chance of making college. It would have been wonderful to continue along the education route, I relished the routine, but Mother was adamant I earn my keep and lined me up with a job stacking shelves down at the supermarket. It would have been bearable if I didn't have to give her three-quarters of my wages towards the bills. The rest I saved under my mattress, until the old witch found my stash and took it. She said she needed it for food, but I drew my own conclusions after finding a hypodermic needle under the sofa. The only decent meal I ever got was on my school dinner ticket. I wasn't so careless again. By the time I was seventeen. I had saved up enough money in a watering can hidden in the garden shed to pay the deposit on my own bedsit. Call me a coward for not standing up to her, but I ran the moment her eyes were averted and I've never looked back.

It's just a single room, with a communal shower in the hall and a toilet that smells putrid, but it's mine. I don't have a video machine for the reruns or one of those electronic cake mixers I've seen advertised on TV. I use a handheld whisk to bake my favourite chocolate muffins. Our lives are surrounded by gadgets we tell ourselves we need but have lived centuries without. Me, I get by with a two-ring hob and my black and white portable. I'm a girl of simple pleasures, although I suppose my second-hand computer makes me a hypocrite.

I've been looking after myself since I was out of nappies. I can cook a mean beans on toast when I want to; just a splash of Worcestershire sauce to give it a kick. Mostly, I eat sandwiches. Mother constantly served me jam on bread, and all these years later, I can't shake off my love for the damn things.

I eat my dinner overlooking the block of flats opposite my building, but sometimes the white bread sticks in my throat. The man often on the first floor does obscene things to himself, and the young kids on the fourth floor are a pair of rips. Their dad tries to knock some sense into them, but I think there are better ways to discipline than using the back of your hand.

When I was in my early twenties, I hit a rough patch. I'd just begun a new job in a supersized supermarket next to my estate and a man came through my checkout and asked my name.

'Patricia,' I said politely.

After that, he started coming through my checkout every week, taking his time pulling out his wallet to pay for his shopping, lingering longer than was necessary. One day, he held the queue up so long, talking about the weather and asking me about my favourite season during the year, then he leaned over the conveyor belt and in a hushed tone asked me to join him in seeing a movie. I could have just said no but he had that glint in his eye I recognised from the men Mother entertained. I went to pieces and called security. What does he think I am? A piece of meat he can smack around and use for his own sick pleasure?

The panic attacks started after that and I lost my job. Benefits have been my crutch ever since. I don't know how long I'll continue getting my payouts, then I don't know what will become of me. The job centre keeps phoning me to say if I don't turn up to see them, they'll have to advise social services I'm not actively seeking work, which may mean they cut off my lifeline. I've tried telling them I break into a cold sweat whenever I attempt to leave home, but they can be so bloody rude. The government doesn't seem to place too much emphasis on their staff having good communication skills.

I hope everything will be okay. I'm harming nobody from here within my sardine can, keeping myself to myself. The outside world is a dangerous web, full of spiders poised to attack flies like me. There's really no need to venture out. I can even order my groceries over the computer once a month, although the delivery charge is extortionate.

The other worldwide web is truly a remarkable invention. Since I found out about it and managed to get it loaded onto my home computer, I can surf around, popping my head into chat rooms for social conversation. Flights to the farthest corners of the earth are at the touch of my fingertips; even though I'll never set foot on an aeroplane. A girl can dream. A rare edition of *Sgt Pepper's Lonely Heart Club* on vinyl can be purchased by Beatles fanatics like me and paid for online to be shipped the next working day. The Internet is a miracle.

Then again, some people can hack into your bank and empty the account, sell their bodies online to the highest bidder, or view sickening child pornography if they are of a twisted mind. The Internet is a monster.

The web creates addicts. People who once devoured the morning paper while eating egg and soldiers for breakfast now log on first thing, forget how to read, and go hungry until dinner time. Others live in squalor, overlook getting dressed and ignore the dishes piling up in the sink while they get tangled up in endless search strings and google cookies. Decent folk who remembered their friends now fail to recall where the post office is and contact only those who supply an email address. And for the worst users like me, those with unlimited broadband allowing twenty-four-hour surfing with no hidden charges, sleep deprivation is as inevitable as rain in Scotland.

Everyone has their vices. Mine are the computer and my programs on the box. My doctor says I have other problems too, what with being a sardine and all. I daresay she's probably right. At times, I think I'm losing my mind. I struggled to trust her initially, but she seems the helpful type, with kindly eyes that crinkle at the sides. I'm starting to look forward to her visits here. They leave me with hope for a better future and optimism to face each day. Eventually, I might be strong enough to confront my demons. It would be wonderful to find the courage to go outside again one day.

The program I'm watching is interrupted by the sound of the doorbell ringing and I drag myself off the sofa with a sigh. Peeking through the eyehole is always a prerequisite in my neighbourhood, if you want to avoid a thug fleecing your home. I lean in to look at my visitor, expecting to see the doctor standing there. She's due to drop by today. I jerk back in fright. Mother is poised on the other side of the door, leopard-print handbag in her grip. I can't comprehend the mixed emotions sending signals to my brain: turmoil, shock, anxiety. There is nobody around to tell me what to do. To advise me if I should open the door or bolt up. How she found me is anyone's guess. Mother has always been cunning.

There is nowhere to run and nobody to turn to. Sick as it is, Mother is my only family. I wrap my fingers around the door handle and clutch the bronze metal until my knuckles go white. She raps again, so hard I jump. A torrent of verbal abuse seeps into my sanctuary through the keyhole. Her bite has left scars on my skin, but this bark of hers is unbearable. She hurt me badly in places you can't see.

I slide the bolt into place, push the armchair against the door, and sink to the floor, rocking, rocking, rocking.

Her fist pounds, louder and louder, flesh on wood. I put my hands over my ears and try not to cry.

I can never leave this house. This will always be my sardine tin. She is out there and I am cooped up in here. Life stinks.

This is not daytime TV. This is my reality.

Creep

'What's your favourite song? Yana asks.

'"Creep" by Radiohead,' I tell my best friend.

It's always on at home. The mellow acoustic version, playing softly in the morning before work. Blaring through surround sound when Wayne is having a beer. I sometimes even hear the faint lyrics emanating from his headphones after we have a fight. It's our song.

Yana raises her eyebrows in a silent stare.

I play dumb. 'What?'

'Your favourite song. Not his?'

'I dunno,' I murmur, taking a sip of white wine.

'What are you going to do?'

I shrug, feeling the blush of hot cheeks.

I popped in to see Yana after work and ended up staying longer than planned. Wayne will be cheesed off I'm out late, but Yana already had pasta ready and a bottle of Chardonnay open when I arrived.

'That's three in a row. Favourite song, favourite restaurant, favourite thing to do on a weekend.'

'So stop asking impossible questions!'

'When did you lose yourself?' Yana asks.

Tears well up in my eyes. 'The day I met him.'

*

It's dark in the bar where I'm having a drink with my big brother. I keep him company while he's trying to make a name for himself as a guitarist at every open mic night around the city. The stools along the counter are occupied by men of all ages sipping pints. Several have leather jackets on.

A couple have instrument cases propped up next to them. There's a microphone up front and a white-haired pensioner is crooning Sinatra as if his life depended on it. When he's done, another singer wearing a cowboy hat and tight jeans steps up. I'm won over from the first husky note of 'Creep'. By the time he climaxes with a gritty ripped up acoustic of Paul Young's 'Wherever I lay my hat', I'm in love.

*

I slip my heels off at the front door and tiptoe through the house to the bathroom. I open the mirrored cabinet and take out my make-up remover from the left-hand side to clean my face. On the opposite side, Wayne's products line the shelf. It still feels strange, sharing my place with someone I've only known a few months. There was no conversation about him moving in. The detachment just hurt like hell whenever he left, so I didn't bother complaining when his stays became longer until they eventually blended into one half of a bathroom cabinet. Nobody could have prepared me for the whirlwind of intense love. The raw nerve ends from an electric touch. A fierce loyalty smoking from an inner fire ignited by passion.

My favourite song used to be 'I'm Every Woman' by Chaka Khan – an anthem for female empowerment. My favourite restaurant was the tiny Italian down the back lane behind Yana's flat. My favourite thing to do was hang out at open mic nights, until Wayne told me they were no place for a girl like me.

I close the cabinet and jump as his reflection looms over my shoulder. He takes off his hat and hooks it over the cold tap.

I didn't lose myself.

He took me.

The day he lay down his hat and took my home.

Red Balloons

I twirl in my white frock with the red sash, the one Dad bought me for my seventh birthday just before he died. I wish he was here to see how nice I look.

'You're my Kitty Kat.' He'd wrap his strong arms around me, throw me up in the air and catch me again.

But he isn't here, Frank is, and Frank has arms like thin, pasty spaghetti. He's waving them about over there, playing air drums to the song being hammered out by the band on stage with a singer who is wearing blue eyeshadow and a shirt with frilly sleeves. Mum looks pretty in her wedding dress, dancing next to him. The front bit of her perm is sprayed stiff over her forehead, with the rest of her dark curls loose right down her back. I wish Mum would let me grow my hair long just like hers.

'Cool song,' says Coleman. He lives opposite our house and he loves singing out loud.

I join in the chorus with him, even though I don't properly know the words yet. Something about a chameleon that comes and goes. I want to ask Coleman what a chameleon is but I don't want him to think I'm a dummy.

'Karma, karma, karma, karma, karma…'

Dancing is making me hot and my mouth is dry. As the band slows to cover a song about Vienna, I wander over to Mum, who now has her perm snuggled in next to Frank's mullet as she sways along with him.

'I'm thirsty.' I gently tug at Mum's white lace dress.

'Little girls are meant to be seen, not heard.'

I stumble away, cutting across the community hall, through the flashing lights that are making patterns on the dance floor like the ones my red kaleidoscope goggles make. Coleman sticks his tongue out as I pass him to reach the round table in the corner with the cake on top. There are chairs either side of it with red balloons tied to them. Everywhere you look, there are so many red balloons, maybe ninety-nine of them. So many the plastic chairs might float to the ceiling. If I tie every one of them to my red sash, maybe there will be enough to carry me right up to heaven to visit Dad. He will be excited to see me; his eyes will crease and his mouth will turn up. Both of us will laugh as he tickles me under the chin.

Plonking myself on the floor, I shuffle on my bum until I'm hiding beneath the cloth covering the trestle table.

Coleman and my best friend, Tash, lift the curtain to crawl in.

'Boo,' says Coleman.

'Leave me alone.'

'No way, Kitty. This den is cool,' he replies.

'Go away,' I say, because he can be so irritating.

Coleman thinks everything is cool. His new train set, Mum's wedding, the song that I don't know the words too about the chameleon.

'What's the matter?' Tash moves into the centre of the den to link arms with me.

'I hate everyone.'

'You don't hate us,' Coleman points out.

I ignore him and turn to Tash. 'Mum won't even get me a drink. All she cares about is Frank.'

'Let's look at the cake instead,' says Coleman.

In a single file, we creep back out to gather around the table.

'Wow!' Coleman says. 'It's like that old couple's garden at the bottom of the street.'

He's not often right, but he's right about Mum's cake. The bakery deserves a gold star for the tower of white iced bricks with red roses spread all over it.

'There's no knife. That's not cool. Don't need one, though.' Coleman scoops a handful of cake from the bottom layer and shoves it into his mouth.

'No! Someone will notice,' I yell, feeling like he's burst me like one of those balloons he's stuck a pin into.

Coleman gawps at me, cake smudged right up to his dimples.

'Maybe we can hide the gap.' Tash lifts a big round circle of creamy cheese from the posh display of cheese and crackers. 'This could work.'

'Cool.' Coleman grabs another handful of cake, splitting it into three pieces to share with me and Tash.

Swallowing my portion quickly, I lick strawberry jam from my fingers.

'You do it, Dumbo.' Tash passes the cheese to Coleman.

I watch his hands at work, moulding it like plasticine. He shapes and smooths the cheese so that it levels perfectly with the cake. Even though he can be annoying, and he says 'cool' a lot, I once saw Coleman build a whole car from Meccano, so he's very good with making things.

'Katherine!'

The wiry frame of Mum descending on us catches me by surprise. Everybody jumps because the band have started singing that Van Halen song, but I jump for real. She only uses my full name when I'm in trouble.

'Leave it, Sylvia, and dance with me.' Frank's pint of beer wobbles in his hand and splashes onto my dress.

'After I've dealt with this one.' Mum yanks my arm, glaring at Coleman and Tash as she tugs me away.

As I turn to look back at them, Coleman tucks his hands in his pockets and walks away. I hate him.

Maybe the band will pump out another song that Mum likes so much she forgets all about the cake. She clenches my wrist and pulls me so roughly towards the toilets my shoes skim the dance floor.

'Ouch!'

'Hurry up!'

I silently beg Jesus to make sure there's a queue of people waiting to pee.

Mum pushes open the door and shoves me inside.

The cubicles all stand empty.

*

I clench my teeth together. Tears mingle with snot as I wipe my face with the back of my hand.

'Keep…still…and…hold…your…dress…up,' Mum says, hitting me with every word.

I hitch my dress to my belly button and try to stop moving, but every whack makes my muscles spasm. I close my eyes and think of the ninety-nine red balloons again and how I want them to help me float away.

Then the beating stops.

'Stop snivelling.' Mum turns to the mirror, patting her hair and grimacing like big people do when they're checking there isn't anything caught in their teeth.

I suck back the rest of my tears and try to get my breathing to return to normal.

'One for luck.' Mum turns to dish out one last, unexpected blow, right across the back of my leg.

The sting to my thigh burns hot and the urine running down onto the floor does nothing to cool it down.

'Clean yourself up,' Mum says, before leaving me alone in the toilets.

I turn my bottom towards the mirror above the sink and crane my head to see how bad the imprints are on my body, but I'm too short to see. Nothing sharp has been used so I know there won't be any blood, but I'm sure there will be a bruise.

I gather a handful of paper towels and wipe up the mess from the floor, then I let my dress fall back to my knees.

Nobody will see the marks. Not Tash. Not Coleman. Not anyone. It's my secret.

Invisible, like the air inside the red balloons.

Pac-Man

A bang next door made her splash Earl Grey everywhere. Nina used the cuff of her jumper to absorb it before the hot tea seeped into her keyboard and caused a malfunction. The neighbours' voices on the other side of the plasterboard were so loud she could hear every word of their abusive language. They were tearing shreds off each other again. Martin was accusing Larissa of wearing an indecently short skirt.

'Hey, Pac-Man, play my favourite grunge tunes,' Nina ordered.

Pac-Man was a wireless smart speaker with several extra dimensions of functionality. Her customisations made the virtual assistant the smartest on the block. Pac-Man analysed her request and sprang to attention, pumping out the gravelly tones of Chris Cornell. The version was a perfect acoustic rendition of 'Black Hole Sun'. The Soundgarden singer-songwriter was her hero. A talented lyric writer with the added bonus of a near four-octave vocal range that made her want to weep. The news of his suicide had been devastating, but his legacy would linger forever.

Nina wondered what legacy she would leave behind when she died. Not that she wanted to quit breathing any time soon. She was only in her mid-twenties; a singleton, living alone in a London flat at the end of a narrow lane decorated with vibrant street art. There was so much she wanted to do in this lifetime. One day, she would make her millions, perhaps by developing something as shallow as a foolproof online dating site, with algorithms executed to perfection. Its search and match functionality would be so accurate it would guarantee an introduction to the man of her dreams and send them off for a candlelit dinner followed by mind-blowing sex. The whole saga would end with a white wedding at a historical castle, then they would enjoy a picture-perfect honeymoon holed up in a ridiculously remote five-star boutique hotel in the heart of the Scottish Highlands.

Her romantic dream was interrupted by the sound of yelling next door, so loud even Chris Cornell couldn't drown out the ruckus. She tapped away on her keyboard, batching new information to synchronise with Pac-Man later.

The black nail polish on her short nails was chipped from spending so many hours on the computer, but she didn't care. Beauty maintenance was a chore. Her blonde hair was cropped, and her face was make-up free, so she could spend every spare minute testing the boundaries of her multitude of smart speakers. Her technology obsession with voice-controlled gadgets had morphed into an addiction since purchasing the first elementary model to take the electronics industry by storm. It had been straightforward enough to use a relatively simple programming language to extend the base logic. Gradually, she moved onto constructing more complex frameworks that superpowered the device so it would respond more astutely to her requests. She learned about the nuances of computer chips. microphones and software that listened and interpreted specific commands. She'd bought a second interactive speaker, manufactured by a different brand, then another.

Google Home was her preference for playing music and tuning into her favourite shows on TV. Amazon Echo responded to the name Alexa and had the uncanny ability of being able to organise her shopping list to her work commitments. Each had their strengths, but none raised her eyebrows as high as Pac-Man.

Pac-Man was her favourite inanimate flatmate. It had been easy to name him. Just like the computer game, he gobbled everything around him with incredible speed. She'd encoded a deeply seductive male voice into him to bring him to life and expanded his brain until it was so large it made her week at the knees. Pac-Man obeyed her every command, keeping her busy until the sun rose and it was time to head into work for her early shift.

*

Nina hated the desk job. A year ago, she'd monopolised the treadmill at gym to ensure she was fit enough to beat the bleep test, because she wanted to join the police force to solve crimes. When she was accepted into the training academy, the euphoria had been indescribable. There was no sorrow in leaving behind the insurance firm where she'd been crunching data since leaving school, finding loopholes in the small print to enable her employer to decline payouts. It was time for her to give back to the world.

When she'd joined the police, she'd started out with high aspirations of gathering enough evidence to put away the monsters who murdered and maimed. She had a logical brain, perfect for analysing evidence, yet here she was, wasted in a humdrum existence, assigned to logging driving offences, monitoring stolen vehicles, and tracking information about serial joyriders. Less than a fortnight into the job, she'd realised there was an underlying trend in the car types that were magnets to thieves. Older models without an immobiliser were common targets for young offenders who relished spinning the wheels to achieve a dope burnout. Utes were the preferred choice by professional robbers, who used them to ram jewellery stores or stripped them down into spare parts to distribute in shipping containers to buyers on the black market.

Then there was the rise in disappearances of the lacklustre four-door sedan. Keys were going missing from suburban homes weeks before the car was whisked away for a one-way drive. These unexplainable mysteries were Nina's favourite. She gained enormous satisfaction from peeking beneath the bonnet to find some shred of evidence hidden from the naked eye.

'What ya got?' Ben, her supervisor, asked over Nina's shoulder, making her jump.

'Plates are being traded from a backstreet outfit in Tottenham, but I've traced it to a national racquet.'

'Good work.' Ben took a bite from a jam doughnut.

'You gotta quit eating those or you'll end up a cliché with a fat gut and a cholesterol problem.'

He put a plate down in front of her with a glazed ring doughnut on it. 'Touché.

'Thanks, boss.'

He wandered off, licking his fingers, and Nina took a bite of hers. The sugar hit immediately worked wonders for her typing, which took on double speed. She punched in registration details, looked up car makes and models, and scrolled through Vehicle Identification Numbers. Making sense of the clues was like solving a major crossword; she eliminated anything that didn't fit the profile and worked methodically through the various sequences until the right answer was obvious.

She worked through her cases swiftly and grabbed a tea break. Earl Grey in an oversized mug with Minnie Mouse on the front and a chipped handle. Her British heritage told her the right thing to do would be to sip her tea in a porcelain cup, held daintily with her little finger sticking out, but she liked to be a rebel.

Ben wandered over again as she was finishing the last of her cuppa. 'You nailed it today, Nina.'

'Thanks.'

'You gotta stop working so fast, though. The rest of the crew can't keep up with you.'

'Give me something different to do then,' suggested Nina, taking Minnie Mouse to the sink and rinsing her out.

'We'll merge you into another team eventually, but you've got to finish your stint in this department. Rules are rules.'

Nina turned to stare at Ben. 'Merging and rules. You're a genius!'

'What are you talking about?'

'It's nothing. Not yet, anyway.' Nina turned the tap off.

Ben shrugged. 'You know, if it were up to me, I would have you skip rank and promote you straight to sergeant.'

Nina gave him a grin before heading back to her cubicle. She couldn't wait for her shift to be over so she could clock out. Not a minute too soon of course. Rules were rules.

*

Harsh wind stung her face as she walked home from the London Underground station. Her place was located above a twenty-four-hour restaurant that served Peruvian food to customers sitting at colourful wooden tables. The enticing smell of cooking filled her nostrils as she wandered down the lane. She'd ate in the place a few times. It was pricy, but the food was delicious. The rocoto dish had a fantastic kick to it. Hot chillies stuffed with spiced beef, onions, olives, and egg white. The restaurant covered them with cheese and milk before baking them into a mouth-watering delight that assaulted the senses.

Ignoring her growling stomach, she avoided temptation to pop in for a top-notch meal. Instead, she let herself in the main door to her apartment block and headed up the stairwell. As she turned a curve on the landing, she slammed into Martin from the flat next door.

'Watch it!'

'Sorry.' Nina gave him an apologetic smile.

Martin stormed past. Tall and sinewy, he was a brute, with a hoop through his upper lip and a phoenix tattoo wallpapering half his neck. A stench of stale cigarette smoke wafted from him. He oozed a fiery ugliness, far more potent than a stuffed rocoto. His presence was an assault on the senses too, but the type that left a bad taste in the mouth.

She hurried to her apartment. Once inside, she opened her fridge and found a Tupperware filled with leftover pasta that had sprouted fur. Tossing it to one side, she moved to the larder and raided the contents for two-minute noodles instead. The kettle was a quarter full, so she boiled it quickly, efficient in the use of time and electricity, then she settled at her desk with the steaming noodles and opened her laptop.

She logged on, her lengthy password a blend of capitals, small letters, numbers and symbols. The combination had been randomly selected and memorised. Not a date of birth, first pet or mother's maiden name in sight. Her desktop sprang into action and she navigated to the file she wanted to work with. It contained information she had been gathering and analysing, relating to dates and times when various real-life domestic violence incidents had occurred. Some information had been gleaned from snippets of conversation between cops in the corridor at work. Other detail was more speculative, about potential triggers for incidents, weapons that might be used to commit an offense, and potential reasons for a peaceful household to suddenly blow up. Jealousy, financial pressure, protracted periods of unemployment, desperation when a partner threatened to leave… They were all common triggers to set off an abuser. In the next file was a long list of rules relating to the law around alcohol consumption, jail terms and rehabilitation regulations. Her fingers moulded into the keys, human and machine at one as they discovered unique ways to handle and process large amounts of data.

When Ben mentioned merges and rules, he had given her an idea. She began to merge her own bank of information. Two files fused into one, then a third, and fourth, until the whole lot sat in one dormant volcano. All she cared about was the sequence in which she processed information and the artificial intelligence algorithms she constructed.

Patterns and predictions.

Probabilities and assumptions.

The wonders of Big Data.

When she was finally done programming, analysing and testing, she fed the entire lot into Pac-Man.

'Hey, Pac-Man…'

Nina posed the curve ball question of all questions. The red light flashed in a flurry of activity on the top of the speaker. It was taking longer than usual to spit out any information. Perhaps she had spoon-fed him too fast and he was unable to digest the concoction of ingredients she had stuffed into him. Nina poised herself for his sexy British voice replying, 'Sorry. I do not understand the question.'

Pac-Man spoke. '28 January, 23.00.'

Nina dropped her fork.

The date was tomorrow.

*

Nina phoned in sick the next day. It was a first for her. Always the diligent employee, arriving ten minutes before her shift, leaving well after it was rostered to finish. But she'd been up all night with Pac-Man, expanding on her algorithms, punching in updates and running various sequences of queries. The hours had sped by while patrons of the Peruvian restaurant wandered up and down the lane, no doubt seeking out classics like the *chicharrón de chancho*: fried pork served with sweet potato. From the window in front of her desk, she could see the trade coming and going at all hours.

Nina ate toast and washed it down with more Earl Grey. There was no time for à la carte menu choices. Pac-Man was keeping her busy.

The device never swayed from telling her what would happen at eleven p.m. tonight.

All Nina had to do was wait.

*

At ten fifty p.m., Nina heard the door slam next door. She stopped pacing around her living room and sat on her sofa. Her hands tugged at the sleeves of her black jumper, stretching the fabric over her fists. The television was on mute, beaming *Sky News*, the time displayed on the right-hand corner of her screen. The hypnotic digits addictively drew her in, making it impossible to tear her eyes away. Then, at ten fifty-nine p.m., a wave of nausea washed over her and she could no longer watch. Her eyes screwed shut, waiting for it to happen.

'Bitch,' she heard Martin yell from next door.

He was a goddamn bully. Squashing Larissa under his thumb. Interrupting the neighbourhood peace. Invading her living room. Consuming the air.

Silence descended on her flat. *Sky News* told her it was 11.01 p.m. She turned the television off. Someone in the lane downstairs smashed a bottle and she almost wet her pants. She got up and looked out the window. A group of three intoxicated males stumbled along and the turned out of the lane into the city grid. A different figure in a black hoodie was spraying the AC/DC slogan on the brick wall a couple of properties away. They had good taste.

The sound of furniture scraping along the floor next door made her cringe. She wondered if Larissa had been shoved against something. A torrential onslaught of vile verbal abuse began again. It lasted several minutes, building up into a crescendo of loud sex.

Nina picked up her phone and called Ben. 'I need you to come over.'

'It's not a booty call, is it?'

Not on my front, no, but I can't speak for next door.'

'Huh?'

'Just come over.' Nina cut him off and tossed her phone down.

'Pac-Man, I need more information.'

The red lights flashed again.

*

By the time Ben got there, the neighbours were quiet again.

'What took you so long?' Nina asked, as she swung open the front door.

'Good evening to you too. Don't you ever unwind?'

Nina shrugged, not at all embarrassed to still be in her police uniform. 'I want to show you something.'

She ignored his look of surprise when he walked into the lounge and spotted the triple monitors, spaghetti junction of cables, and plethora of smart speakers.

'What the… Are you running NASA out of here?'

'Just listen.' She cleared her throat. 'Pac-Man, when will Martin physically abuse Larissa.'

The red lights flashed. '29 January, 21.45.'

'Who are Martin and Larissa?' Ben asked.

'My neighbours. They've been rowing for weeks and it sounds way more aggressive than it used to. Yesterday, I asked Pac-Man when they would next have a fight and he told me it would be tonight. The exact time, Ben. Pac-Man knew the precise moment they would kick off.'

'Are you saying your home device can predict domestic violence incidents?'

'Exactly.'

Ben laughed, one of his big rumbling guffaws which Nina loved. He was funny and warm-hearted; married of course, but all the good ones were.

'I'm serious, Ben.' She launched into a stream of technical jargon, making Ben hold his hand up.

'Stop! You lost me at the predictive mapping and software statistics bit.'

'I'm saying you should believe Pac-Man. You heard what he said. At 21.25 tomorrow night, there will be yet another punch up next door.'

Ben ran his hands through his hair. 'And what do you expect me to do about a crime that hasn't happened yet?'

'That's for you to figure out.'

*

The following night, Ben arrived at Nina's flat armed with Chinese takeaway.

'How can you stomach food at a time like this?' Nina asked, as Ben settled on the sofa and began to tuck in.

'I've got plenty of time to eat before the action starts.'

'Fifteen minutes.'

'Like I said, plenty of time.'

Nina shook her head and went back to injecting Pac-Man with a plethora of advanced instructions. An ever-changing technology ecosystem was available online. She linked the device to geospatial techniques, GPS data, insights, and publicly available datasets. Pac-Man was eating up a wealth of knowledge at an incomprehensible speed while she used complex analytics to make sense of it all. In return for her undivided attention, Pac-Man was producing mind-boggling responses, with his level of coherent accuracy improving by the minute.

'Are you sure these neighbours of yours are home?' Ben asked.

'Yep, they had the television on…' Nina paused as an almighty crash sounded from next door. 'They must go through dozens of plates a week.'

'How come you've never tried to intervene, Nina? I mean, you're a cop.'

'A month ago, I stopped by when I knew he was out. Larissa told me to mind my own business and slammed the door in my face. I've tried twice more since then. Same thing.'

'You serious?'

'Some people don't want the help. Until recently, their fights honestly didn't seem too bad. I thought they were just a hot-headed pair having more than their fair share of lovers' tiffs. Lately, though, I've begun to seriously worry about her safety.' Nina shut her laptop and wandered over to sit in the maroon armchair opposite Ben. 'So, what do we do?' Can we arrest him?'

'No. We're going to wait.'

'Wait for what?'

For next time.

*

Nina lay in bed that night, tossing and turning between the sheets, insomnia her only companion. She'd let Pac-Man relax in standby mode after grilling him on when next time would be. After Ben had gone home, she'd felt dismayed her supervisor wanted to let Larissa be subjected to another beating just so he could be sure Pac-Man's predictions were more than a lucky one-off.

'Technology is prone to glitches,' he'd said.

Nina knew this was true if the coding was not perfect. Sloppy work could lead to an incomprehensible jumble of nonsense, but she'd been meticulous in every interaction with the machine. He was an obedient student who listened intently. His mistakes were infrequent, and he learned from them, so next time he knew better. She treated Pac-Man with respect, feeding his insatiable appetite with more information until he was so fat he was simply bursting to come out with predictions.

Ben thought it was a fluke.

Nina knew it was only the beginning.

*

It took three more occurrences of domestic violence next door before Ben took Nina seriously and escorted her and Pac-Man in to see the big boss.

The chief superintendent did not take half as long as Ben to be convinced about Pac-Man's capability. 'This is real-life Minority Report stuff. I heard they trialled a similar initiative in Scotland Yard. They were testing software designed to search social media profiles and interrogate photographic imaging using facial recognition techniques. Various experiments were going on, using algorithms to map out criminal networks and to make sense of petabytes of unprocessed data they had gathered relating to suspects. The programme was supposed to disrupt the whole way they did their police investigations, reducing the manual processing time of information relating to their cases. I believe they also wanted to use similar technology to put details of jailed criminals through an electronic risk assessment to see if they would reoffend again if they were paroled.'

'And did it work?' Nina asked.

'Dunno. They had a whole army of technology geeks working on it until they lost their funding. There are so many cutbacks across the public sector there's not a penny left for the police to innovate. Nothing like this has ever been trialled in the Met, though. It's too radical for the London bigwigs to invest in. How on earth did you manage to work on such a big project? Have you had any assistance?'

Nina shook her head. 'No, sir. It's just stuff I've been tinkering with.'

'Good grief. Are you a prodigy of some kind?'

'I just enjoy maths, sir. And I'm not too bad with a computer, I suppose.'

'She's being modest. Nina is totally one of those technology geeks you're referring to,' Ben said.

'Show me,' instructed the chief superintendent.

Nina set the smart speaker down on his desk. 'Pac-Man, when will Martin next physically abuse Larissa?'

Pac-Man flashed his red lights and the chief superintendent cleared his diary for the day.

*

The demonstration caused a whirlwind of activity to swallow Nina whole. First, the chief superintendent made her sign a non-disclosure agreement, so she could view sensitive cases relating to abusive households. Next, she was told she was off the desk job. No more stolen cars to track down.

The chief superintendent's initial thoughts were for Nina to continue developing Pac-Man inside the police headquarters, but he changed his mind after pondering on the IT security red tape he would need to cut through just to secure approval for Pac-Man to be plugged in for a recharge of the batteries.

'Let's keep this under wraps until we have a decent proof of concept documented and proven. We don't want to kick up a hornet's nest until we're ready,' he said. 'This smart speaker is your own personal home equipment, right?'

'Right,' Nina agreed.

'So take it back home and keep doing what you're doing. I'm going to give you a backup drive containing confidential information about a case I'd like you to look at. The drive contains evidence which should not be leaving this office. Do you understand what I'm saying?'

'Yes, sir.'

'And organise a locksmith to increase the security on your flat.'

Nina realised his concern was justified. The police force had taught her a thing or two about self-defence, so it wasn't a physical attack from someone like Martin that would be of threat to her. It was a stranger sneaking in to come for Pac-Man. There were lots of crafty people out there who might stumble upon what she was developing. People like her, who had learned to hack as a childhood hobby and could tiptoe through the online world undetected. A gadget as smart as Pac-Man, with embedded lines of intricate code and supernatural capability, would attract attention. This was a device unrecognisable from its original store-bought form; a chatbot with a unique, super-sized, artificially intelligent brain. He was an attractive target; the technology equivalent of a Lamborghini to car thieves. In the wrong hands, and with some reverse engineering, Pac-Man would be able to predict and advise criminals exactly where the nearest policeman was. Even worse, it could be used to notify drug dealers if their port drop would be next in line for a spot check, or to alert terrorist cells if the walls were closing in on them.

'I'll have Ben roster you onto a few days personal leave, to give you a head start,' said the chief superintendent.

A head start on what, sir?'

'On using Pac-Man to see if it can figure out something more serious.'

'Could you give me an example of what you mean by serious, sir?'

'Murders. I want you to solve murders.'

*

The minute she got home, Nina plugged the portable hard drive into her laptop and began applying her algorithms to the mega amounts of historical data it contained. The hard drive contained three years of records relating to an old domestic violence case which had ended with a woman, by the name of Hannah Angelo, on a slab in the morgue. On six different occasions before she died, Hannah had been admitted to hospital with broken bones. Twice, the police had been summoned to her property by concerned neighbours hearing an argument. In one particularly nasty incident, Hannah's husband had ended up being formally cautioned for giving her a black eye. There had been a public outcry afterwards at how the authorities had failed to connect the dots and intervene before it was too late.

Nina transmitted and merged information about the Hannah Angelo case from the police records with her own dormant volcano of rules, predictions, assumptions, and insights, finally loading everything through Pac-Man. The only thing she excluded was detail of when the woman's life abruptly came to an end. Instead, she asked Pac-Man to predict the moment her life would come to an end. This time, Pac-Man didn't hesitate. He confirmed the time and date Hannah Angelo would be beaten to death. The exact time her husband had taken a cricket bat to her head as if trying to knock a six out of the park.

Nina called Ben.

Ben called the chief superintendent.

The chief superintendent called Nina. 'We're both coming over. Don't move an inch.'

Nina made herself a fresh cup of tea. She knew she had built something spectacular. A device that could answer such inconceivable questions she could barely believe it herself. She was poised to take a sip of Earl Grey when an awful possibility entered her head.

'Pac-Man.' Nina paused. 'When will Martin murder Larissa?'

Pac-Man flashed.

Red…

Red…

Red…

He rattled off a date and time.

Nina could barely breathe.

Martin was going to kill Larissa tonight.

*

'I need you to make an arrest,' Nina said, the second Ben and the chief superintendent arrived at her flat.

'Of who?' asked the chief superintendent. The case we gave you is over. Hannah Angelo's husband is behind bars for what he did to her. All I want to know is if your machine methodically processed the data and correctly predicted when the domestic violence would turn into something even more sinister.'

'Yes. Pac-Man knew exactly when Hannah was going to be killed. It's not about that case. It's Martin, my neighbour.'

'Are they fighting again?' Ben asked.

'Not yet, but listen to this.' Nina cleared her throat. 'Pac-Man, when will Martin murder Larissa?'

Pac-Man answered.

Ben's eyes widened. 'Tonight!'

'Hang on a minute. Let's not get carried away with this machine of yours,' said the chief superintendent to Nina.

Nina pushed her shoulders back and jutted her chin. 'With all due respect, sir, if Pac-Man says it's going to happen tonight, trust me, tonight it will be. Surely the fact he correctly predicted the time of the Hannah Angelo murder is enough to convince you.'

'We cannot breathe a word about you reviewing the Hannah Angelo case. It was merely to discreetly test if this Pac-Man of yours had any merit.' The chief superintendent rubbed his stubble. 'There are sensitivities... That data should never have been in your hands.'

'I signed the non-disclosure to ensure all the correct approvals were in place to look at the file.'

'Oh, please, that was merely to ensure you didn't tell your friends about a confidential police case over cocktails. I didn't use it to gain the appropriate permission to go down this path. It's sitting in my top drawer. If this leaks out, we'll have a whole data privacy breach investigation to face. You were given access to secure police records to feed into an unauthorised third-party device, housed outside the station, for crying out loud. It was a huge misjudgement on my part. If the press gets wind of this, or the prime minister…it doesn't bear thinking about.'

'But, sir…' said Nina.

'But nothing. If we arrest Martin, on the basis we think he might kill Larissa, then what? He'll deny ever intending to do such a thing.'

'We have to do something. A lady is in danger.'

'We will do something. We will wait. If Pac-Man is right, and Larissa ends up dead, I'll do everything in my power to secure funding for you to work on artificial intelligence projects that will exceed your wildest dreams. With even more time, maybe Pac-Man can predict not only the date and time of murders, but also the name of the murderer. We could have one of these speakers on every desk in the force.'

'He's right,' said Ben, collapsing on the sofa. 'All Pac-Man has really done is predict a couple of punch-ups between lovers and figured out the date and time of a murder in a case where we already had the answers. We need to prove the artificial intelligence is right about this type of situation, about a murder that has yet to happen, but it has to be done in a controlled way.'

'Pac-Man can't put the cuffs on someone. We have a moral obligation to make sure Larissa is safe.' Nina glared at the two men in front of her, dumbfounded they were willing to let someone die to prove viability of Pac-Man. Once they could prove he was authentic, they would clone and commoditise him. Make more bots that could answer whodunnit questions. But not without covering their backsides first. 'It's up to you both to do the right thing. 'Please, call for back-up, or do something. We're running out of time,' she begged.

The chief superintendent stared at Ben.

Ben stared at Nina.

Nina stared at Pac-Man.

His lights were off as he waited patiently for instructions.

The only sound to be heard was the gunshot next door.

Road Rage

Someone is riding my tail. Why can't he give me some breathing space like a normal courteous driver? I want to see at least thirty metres of tar behind me, not him and his expensive wheels up close and personal. If he gets an inch nearer, I'll be able to see the hairs up his nostrils. S'pose he might not have any hair up there, given he's bald. Not the most attractive fella. Typical. Can't remember the last time an attractive man rode me from behind.

He pushes his spectacles up his nose. They look like jam jars. You'd think there would be enough horsepower in lenses that thick to help him see he's revving too close to my bumper.

Rush hour traffic is horrendous. He better not hit my vehicle. Didn't have enough caffeine this morning to cope with dealing with a dent. I press the button decorated with two red triangles. Hear the clicking as the hazard warning light clicks into action.

On.

Off.

On.

Off.

My eyes dart to the rear-view mirror to watch him back off. Catch him giving me the finger instead. Aggressive asshole. Thinks he owns the road. I curse to myself. He looks like he's muttering something too. Maybe he swore back.

'F**k you.'

Or could be he's a high achiever on a hands-free call, selling over-priced car insurance to bad drivers like himself. Nah, looks like he's singing. Mouth is moving fast and he's jiggling in his seat. Must be a good tune. Perhaps a bit of Michael Jackson. 'Man in the Mirror.' I give him the finger back and switch my radio on.

Snakes and Ladders

Miranda clapped hard as the ball soared through the air and dropped through the metal hoop. She hovered on the sidelines next to Suzy, who was shivering in a purple netball dress made of breathable, micromesh fabric that was too tight for her plump body. Even in the northern suburbs of Western Australia, when it should be warm, the spring weather was occasionally unpredictable. This morning, after a bowl of her favourite cereal, Miranda had used voice command to ask her new smartphone about the Perth forecast. That Siri woman had answered back that the day would be sunny, but she was wrong. There was a bite in the air and a strong breeze was starting to toss leaves down from the trees growing along the far side of the netball court. They were a distraction from play, floating around like green confetti at a wedding. Miranda was glad she'd suspected the smartphone was not as smart as her. She'd been clever enough to bring a jumper along, otherwise she would be shivering like everybody else.

'Go, Collette,' Suzy shouted at the pretty redhead who was team captain.

Miranda loved Collette, who was an outstanding player, but she hated Suzy's high-pitched voice. Suzy sounded like she'd sucked the helium from enough balloons to decorate an eleventh birthday party for every single girl on the Stormtroopers team. Miranda did the right thing and tried to think nice thoughts about Suzy, but nothing came to mind. She was just plain irritating. The way she played with her hair whenever she was substituted, sucking on the end of her stupid inside-out yolk braids. Her prim and perfect mother must spend ages weaving them for her every Saturday morning. And the way she always dragged her left foot when the ball was in her hands. Suzy was a dummy. Everyone else on the team had mastered the basic rule about no stepping with the ball.

'Coach, when can I go back on to play?' Suzy whined from behind the yellow line.

Coach Becky ignored her as she jogged around the perimeter of the court. 'Come on, girls. Tighter. Keep it tighter. You're giving them way too much space.'

Miranda thought Coach Becky should wear army camouflage when she was barking orders at the troops. Even the subs in the trenches were caught up in her commands, waiting to be called upon to fire on the enemy. Coach Becky didn't even let anyone take a toilet break.

The enemy was quick off the mark, their lanky wing defence player intercepting a perfectly decent lob from Collette. The opposition snatched the advantage, covering the length of the court in a flash to take a goal.

Miranda groaned. 'What's the score now, Suzy? It must be close.'

Suzy shrugged, so Miranda narrowed her green eyes. 'Well, go and ask.'

'I can't move. I hurt my foot during that last quarter.'

'When?'

'As I jumped to get that tip to stop them smashing us. That's why Coach Becky took me off.'

'No, it's not. It was just your turn to sit out.' Miranda knew she sounded spiteful, but Suzy needed to toughen up. 'Why do you bother playing when every little knock makes you cry?'

Suzy's mouth started to quiver. Miranda noticed it was also turning blue from the wind. Her lips were wobbling like that tasty blue jelly served at Collette's party last month. Best party ever. The jelly had made every kid in year six resemble an epic Smurf.

Suzy rubbed her foot. 'Coach Becky saw me twist my ankle.'

Miranda rolled her eyes. 'Whatever.'

Two spectating mothers were gorging on their second round of take-away coffees bought from the refreshment van parked beside the umpire's office. They were sitting on canvas foldable camping chairs a few paces from Miranda and Suzy. In between sipping, they kept putting their cardboard cups in the drink holders built into the arms of their camping chairs. Miranda had never liked the posh witches, with their tartan fleece blankets thrown over their stick insect legs.

The half-time whistle blew.

'Oranges time.' Suzy jumped to her feet and skipped over to the team, who were gathering together in a huddle on one side of the court.

Miranda followed with a bounce in her step from her new Air Flex training shoes. 'I thought you said your foot was sore.'

Suzy turned and stared back silently. Miranda hated her googly eyes that were too big for her ugly pixie face.

'Where are the oranges?' Coach Becky asked. 'Who was rostered to bring them?'

Miranda stared in the direction of the posh mothers who had their heads bent in deep conversation. All they ever seemed to gossip about was hairdressing tips or the latest acrylic nail techniques. Even when the team scored, they had a delayed reaction in cheering.

Coach Becky wandered over to Suzy's mum and came back with a pack of snake lollies. 'Unfortunately, there's no fresh fruit today, girls, but you all like snakes, right? A hit of sugar might make you play better.'

Miranda watched Coach Becky open the candy snakes and offer them around the team. Miranda took one last. A green one because all the best red and yellow ones had gone. Then Suzy, who was standing beside her, grabbed a second snake and bit off the tail.

'Greedy,' Miranda said loudly. Fascinated, she watched Suzy's jaw stop moving. There was probably still a piece of mushy lolly in her mouth. The untouched snake head was clenched in Suzy's fist. 'You better eat that bit else your hands will get so gooey the netball will stick to you.'

'I don't want it.' Suzy bowed her soggy braids towards the ground.

Miranda gave a tut. 'Did you know that even when you cut off a snake's head, it can still bite?'

Suzy opened her palm and offered the remainder of her snake to Collette. 'Do you want this?'

'Gross.' Collette screwed her snub nose, then she looked at Coach Becky. 'Why have we not got oranges?'

'Yeah, who else has ever forgotten something so important?' asked Miranda, staring again at the women on the camping chairs. 'I mean, last week I brought oranges and watermelon.'

'Not me!' the girls shouted one by one.

Suzy blushed. 'Mum probably didn't realise it was my turn.'

'It's your fault we've got horrible snakes, so eat it, podgy,' said Miranda.

Suzy lifted the snake head and put it in her mouth.

Miranda put her hands on her hips and watched impatiently as she chewed it slowly as a cow might munch on tasteless grass. 'Next time you should tell your mum to stop worrying so much about buying coffee and to remember to bring oranges.'

'Yeah, Suzy, get your priorities right,' added Collette, before marching off court as it was her quarter to sit out.

'Ouch,' Suzy exclaimed as Miranda walked past too and knocked her.

'Sorry,' said Miranda. 'It was an accident. You better not be a crybaby over it. Let's just get the bibs swapped.'

The team suddenly dived into a scrum, bare arms flying everywhere as they tugged their bibs off. They exchanged them and stuck the new positions onto the Velcro patches on each other's backs.

'Oh, crumbs.' Miranda grimaced when she saw Coach Becky pass Collette's goal attack bib to Suzy. 'There's not much chance of winning this match if we have to rely on her to attack. I hope the team doesn't slide too much further down the ladder.'

Coach Becky glared at Miranda, her mouth hanging open wide. For a moment, Miranda thought Coach Becky was going to say something sharp, but she just stood there, catching flies for dinner.

The single shrill of the whistle cut through the babbling noise from the girls, passing on a message to them to scatter across the court, like one of those gastro bugs that swept through entire school populations quickly. Thinking of bug infestations made Miranda suddenly think of head lice as Suzy fiddled with her braids.

'I hope you haven't got nits,' Miranda shouted to Suzy as the second half of the game began.

'Has Suzy got nits?' Collette called back from the sideline so loudly several players paused in their play.

Miranda nodded.

Collette screwed up her face. 'That's disgusting!'

'Yuk,' said a girl from where she stood, poised in her purple dress on the edge of the semicircle.

'She better not come near me,' the feisty player in centre position said to nobody in particular.

The other team scored another goal, but the Stormtroopers team didn't seem to care. They were far more interested in the news that Suzy might have head lice, which travelled all the way from goal shooter down to goalkeeper and all the way across to the camping chairs.

'My daughter has not got nits!' Suzy's mum shouted, jumping up so fast her coffee flew from the cup holder and spilled down her turquoise, active-wear leggings. 'Who started the nasty rumour that Suzy has got nits?'

Suzy cast a look at Miranda and failed to notice the ball fly towards her from the hands of the wing defence on the opposing team. It smacked her in the nose. The umpire blew hard on her whistle to halt play.

'Blood break! We need the sub,' shouted Coach Becky. 'Collette, that's you. Get ready to come on.'

'Who said she has nits?' bellowed Suzy's mum again.

Suzy sobbed loudly as blood trickled down her face and dripped onto her netball dress. 'Miranda said it first. Then Collette.'

'I did not say Suzy has nits,' said Miranda indignantly.

'Neither did I,' said Collette.

Suzy's posh mum handed a tissue to Suzy and then came up to Miranda. She was so close Miranda could see her nostrils flare. 'You'd better apologise.'

'I will not.'

'This is bullying, Miranda,' said Suzy's mum.

'Don't be such a drama queen,' Miranda retorted. 'Oh, and you've got coffee froth on your lip.'

A red rash crept up Suzy's mum's neck and her eyes bulged. They were exactly like Suzy's huge eyes, only they were surrounded by longer lashes decorated with clumpy mascara.

'I'm only trying to help,' said Miranda.

Suzy dabbed at her nose. 'Mum, I really need to sit down.'

'What a palaver. Give her another snake and she'll be fine,' said Miranda

'This bullying has to stop.' Suzy's mum escorted her daughter off court to swop places with Collette.

Miranda picked up her clipboard and pen to finish assessing the Stormtroopers. 'Bullying. What a drama queen. No girl would dare bully anyone while I'm president of the netball committee!'

Suzy's mum glared at Collette and then at Miranda. 'I don't care who you are. Your daughter is a bully and I know exactly who the snake is she learned it from.'

Miranda put a cross next to Suzy's name on her player evaluation sheet and added a tick next to Collette, her daughter.

The whistle blew, but the game was already lost, and the Stormtroopers slipped down the ladder.

Ruffles

We weren't planning on ending up on this train. The attack came from nowhere. Vultures swooping for the kill.

They saw red. Spot of bother. Had to fly.

I cling on as the train sways in the wind. Panic mounts as I scan the pristine white landscape around me. There's no sign of her anywhere. This whole situation is confusing. Maybe they took her.

Never seeing the love of my life again would leave me with clipped wings. The ability to ever soar again would be stripped away. I'd be crushed underfoot. It's an unbearable thought. I need luck on my side to find my lady.

Today's ruffles are overwhelming. Suffocating my thinking. Preventing me seeing clearly. I need to get off, but I can't. Not without her.

I clamber along the train, frantically checking every crevice. Searching for the unique curves of her body. The beauty of her. She's breathtaking. The kind of lady everyone wants to hold in the palm of their hand because she has that special energy that can change the world from bad to good.

The train slows to a halt. Voices murmur. I can't understand what they are saying. Something about death…until death do us part.

Fear rips through my body. This is it. It's time to jump so I have a chance of survival and can find her. There must be a better vantage point to see this whole train from.

My body twists and turns as I fly through the air. I land on the ground a few metres from the train. I'm alive. I can see everything from here.

Two people are standing together. Him in black. Her in white. Larger than life. There's a blood red spot at the very end of the train.

I flap, hasty to get to my soulmate. Afraid. So afraid she might be injured.

I'm halfway towards the train when she leaps. Then she's beside me, still in one piece. A beautiful miracle. The buzz of excitement is uncontrollable.

We cling together for a moment, watching the man slip a ring on the woman's finger. From a distance, the train on her dress is spectacular. Sparkling diamantes run down a section at the back I hadn't seen before when I was lost in the silky folds. The man in the black suit kisses the woman in the white dress. They're lucky to have found one another.

I'm lucky to have found my ladybird out here in the winelands too, amidst this party of people that invaded our land.

We scan for the vultures that invaded the skies too, but they are nowhere to be seen.

Then I see a red back.

Not red with black spots like us.

Black with one red spot.

The kind of red back that is more dangerous than any vulture, frozen in a web straight ahead.

We fly back towards the safety of the train, where we can hide from the poised spider for a little while.

The Nest

Eliza felt the ache across her lower back as she bent to tape the last of her brown boxes closed. Inside her head she still felt a spring chicken, but her sixty-one-year-old body was beginning to disagree. She straightened up slowly and placed her hands on her hips, staring around the rented house in Kallaroo she'd occupied for the last three decades. It looked completely different without the array of colourful vases decorating each room and her eclectic collection of toby jugs jostling for space on the mantelpiece.

The sound of the removal van pulling up in her drive prompted her to grab the brush to give the laminate floors one final sweep. So much dust to clean up before she handed back the keys to the property agent. She wished she had someone to help her, but since Bobby had passed away of cancer, the many household chores had all fallen on her shoulders. Acute myelogenous leukaemia had spread rapidly through his blood. It had taken him quickly. Collapsed one day in a dizzy spell and gone three weeks later.

Both of her children had flown home to Western Australia to be by her side at their father's funeral, but had since returned to their lives overseas. They were making the most of their university degrees. Tom was in Japan teaching English to high school children, while Clint, her eldest, was on a two-year contract in Hong Kong, working for a construction firm who had been engaged to make ongoing extensions to the Asian Disneyland infrastructure. She didn't begrudge them their freedom. Her boys made her immensely proud. They were so like Bobby, kind souls with unruly dark curls and unwavering commitment to everything they did.

The doorbell rang and she opened the door for the two removal men, both dressed for the occasion in shorts and T-shirts. Much of her furniture had been tossed out on her front lawn a few days ago, free to anyone who wanted to take it. The remainder would be carted away in bulk collection by the City of Joondalup council. Only her good pieces were going with her. The solid mahogany coffee table, with beautiful carved legs, that had been passed down by her mother. Bobby's favourite armchair that she couldn't bear to part with. The bed she'd shared with the love of her life for every one of their forty-one years of marriage. She was downsizing from a four-bedroom rental to finally get on the property ladder with the purchase of her very own two-bedroom apartment in Busselton.

Bobby always loved familiarity and routine. He'd been so comfortable in their rented house he'd never been interested in buying a place of their own. 'Never been in debt and not about to start now,' he had told Judy whenever she had broached the subject of how much money they burned every month to line the pockets of their landlord.

After Bobby died, she'd been forced to review her whole financial situation. She had met with a mortgage advisor, Mr Garrity, from her bank, who had talked her through the process of purchasing her own property and the contractual terms on offer. He told her about a fabulous arrangement where buyers did not want to put down a large deposit, or did not have the cash to do so. The bank offered a full loan of one hundred per cent of the purchase price with mortgage insurance added into the fees. Mr Garrity advised that the costs of the mortgage insurance would be spread over the full tenure of the mortgage, barely affecting her monthly repayments, so she'd gone ahead with this option. It meant she could use her small nest egg of savings to live on.

Leaving behind her large house would be a relief. It was unmanageable, paying high rent to live on her own in such a big old property in the city's northern suburbs. Instead, the smaller new build she was purchasing would be much easier to maintain, and repayments were actually lower than her rent. She adored the compact kitchen with granite tops and an oven that heated up in seconds. Practical for a widow cooking for one. The outdoor balcony was big enough for a small table and chairs, which she planned to surround with pot plants. It would blissful to sit and read romance books written by her favourite local Australian authors. As soon as she'd realised she had a glimpse of the ocean and Busselton jetty, she had known it was perfect. It would be a fresh start. Not that she wanted to forget about Bobby. It was simply more sensible to manage her finances a little more tightly now he was gone. It had been a shock to find out Bobby had let his life insurance lapse the previous year, leaving her to survive only on her savings and government pension. Since he'd passed away, she'd been trying to generate income from doing clothing alterations on her sewing machine at home, but the business had never really taken off. Clothes were so cheap these days, mass produced in China, Taiwan and other exotic places. Most people simply bought new garments and tossed the old and ill-fitting into landfills. Such a wasteful generation.

'That seems to be the last of all the furniture now, Mrs Corbitt,' the removal man said, red in the face as he lugged a bedside table past her. 'A few more boxes to load and that will be us.'

'Good gracious. That was quick. I just realised I need to nip to the cash machine to pay you for today. There's one just on the corner of the street. Will you be all right here without me for a few minutes?'

'Yep, no drama if it means we get paid in cash.'

Eliza pulled on her grey overcoat and grabbed her purse. There was a chill in the air outside, which was unusual for this time of year in Western Australia. Spring was usually so predictable with dry days and breathtaking sunsets along the coastline. Still, it wasn't raining and for that she was grateful. It wouldn't do at all to end up soaked to the bone in the middle of moving to a new house.

She walked briskly down the street, past Norma's house with the perfectly shaped hedge and immaculate lawn that tugged at her heart. Bobby had such green fingers, nurturing plants as he had nurtured her; with care and sustenance. The convenience store on the corner was open all hours and had a built-in ATM on the outer wall that dispersed dollars to all manner of customers. There was no queue today. Sometimes it could be three or four people deep; busier than the post office where she drew her meagre pension. Eliza felt another wave of gratitude that luck was on her side. She had so much to do. Packing up one's life was such a draining experience. It was best to get it all over as quickly as possible.

Eliza inserted her plastic card and punched in her four-digit pin code: the year she married Bobby. The screen prompted her through the necessary steps and her balance popped up on screen. Her heart raced and Eliza put both hands on the ATM to steady herself. Her balance was several thousand dollars overdrawn.

Just last week, all her funds had been in order. Her nest egg of savings was everything she had. Enough to keep her going. To put bread on the table and milk in her many cups of tea. To add to the insult, the machine spat Eliza's card back out in disgust.

Eliza put her card back in her tan leather purse and raced back home. As she approached her drive, she could see both removal men leaning on the van, one tapping away on his mobile phone, the other drinking chocolate chill straight from the carton.

'All done, Mrs Corbitt. We're ready to head to the new place now.' The eldest of them gave her the brightest grin, perfect white teeth shining through his overgrown beard.

'I'm…I'm afraid there's been a misunderstanding.' Eliza could feel the heat burning a path up her cheeks. 'My money… It's all gone.'

'What do you mean, your money? I hope this isn't a sign that our payment is in trouble.' The white teeth disappeared back into the depths of the woolly beard.

Eliza stumbled inside the house, the two men in tow. She grabbed the handset for her landline from where it hung on the wall and dialled the bank.

'Press one for…'

She listened to the confusing options, pressing various combinations, praying for a human to pick up. Accusing stares were being thrown her way from the two men standing in her living room but she could not tell them anything more until she herself knew what the problem was. It took several minutes that seemed like endless hours, before she finally got through to her mortgage manager, Kenneth Garrity.

'How can I help you, Mrs Corbitt?'

Eliza launched into a tirade, her words tumbling over one another as she tried to explain the unusual activity in her savings account.

'Let me bring up the account details,' Mr Garrity told her, his tone calm and assured.

Eliza felt soothed by his composure. The problem would be solved now. Everything would be okay and she could pay these two hovering gentlemen their cash to move her furniture in no time at all.

'Oh, yes. I can see exactly why your account is overdrawn,' Mr Garrity pressed on. 'It's the mortgage insurance fee. The transaction came out of your account this morning to fund the insurance for taking a full loan with no deposit. Everything is in order.'

'Everything is not in order.' Eliza tried to keep her voice from quivering. 'The fee for the insurance was supposed to be spread over the monthly payments over the full twenty-year term of the mortgage.'

'I'm afraid that is not the case, Mrs Corbitt. The mortgage insurance is deducted in one bulk sum on the day of transferring the new property into your name. It applies to all mortgages where the borrower has taken a loan exceeding eighty per cent of the sale price.'

'No, that cannot be true. I specifically asked you about it during our meeting. You told me that all charges applicable to the mortgage would be rolled into my monthly repayments and the mortgage fees would barely make a difference to the amount I pay back every month to the bank. If you recall, we discussed whether it would be better to put down a deposit or take mortgage insurance. You persuaded me to take the mortgage insurance, but did not once mention that twenty thousand would be deducted in a lump sum for it.'

'Now, now, Mrs Corbitt. You may have not fully understood the terms and conditions that you were signing…'

'I read my contract thoroughly and there was not a word about this one-off deduction in there.'

'Well, that is more than likely because it's standard procedure to take the full cost of the mortgage insurance from the customer on transfer day. It is nothing unusual, Mrs Corbitt.'

'Stop!' Eliza yelled. 'Just stop. How can you say this is not unusual? We are not talking about a ten-dollar fee for a bounced cheque. This is everything I have. My life savings. I would have been better off paying the deposit rather than this situation. You have wiped out every dollar from my account without my explicit permission and I certainly did not sign up anywhere for this. May I please speak to your supervisor?'

'I'm afraid that won't be possible. The branch manager is off today. I can schedule a callback, tomorrow?'

'Tomorrow is no good. I have bills to pay today. I have removal men waiting here with my furniture. What am I supposed to do?'

'I'm terribly sorry, Mrs Corbitt. There's nothing I can do.'

Eliza hung up. Her whole body was trembling. 'I…I don't know what to say…'

'Sounds like a rough situation,' the bearded removal man said, his face softening in concern. 'Look, let us get moving with this furniture and we can sort out payment later. I can see this is a difficult day for you.'

'Oh, my, thank you. I promise you will get everything I owe. I just need time to sort things out with the bank.' Eliza sobbed. She wished her comfortable sofa was there to sink onto. Her legs wanted to give way at the kindness being shown to her from this strange man, which was far more than her own bank had shown her.

'Don't let the bastards get you down,' the removal man said, before disappearing down the passage with his colleague.

Eliza sat down on the floor, head in hands. She missed Bobby more than ever. What a mess. She couldn't even begin to think about the rest of her bills. They would mount up in no time. It was the kind of situation where a cup of tea was needed, but the kettle was gone. She didn't even have enough money in her purse to nip to the tea room down the road. positioned right next door to the convenience store and that wretched ATM machine. A cup of tea solved so many problems, but even that was out of reach.

The tears fell, hard and fast, then she wiped her eyes with the handkerchief she kept tucked up the sleeve of her knitted jersey. She pulled herself up off the floor, took a deep breath, and pulled her shoulders back. No good wasting another moment rolling around in her own self-pity.

'If you're almost ready to leave, I'll lock up behind you,' Eliza said as the removal men finished packing the last couple of boxes. 'There's something I need to do which might help with this whole ridiculous mess.'

'Sure. We'll meet you there.'

Eliza watched the van pull away, then did one final stroll around the empty property. This had been her home for so many years and it filled her with happy memories. To have enjoyed such wonderful years with Bobby and the boys was a blessing. Eliza smiled, and then walked out. She closed the door softly behind her and locked it for the last time.

The walk to the library was not far. Ten minutes at a brisk pace. Doreen was on the front desk when she got there.

'Eliza, hello. I wasn't expecting to see you. I thought you were moving today.'

'I am. It's just a quick stop and it's not for new books to loan. Do you mind if I have a cup of tea? I'm parched and it will help me think.'

'Of course.' Doreen nodded towards the new hot drinks machine installed last month. 'That machine is the best investment the council ever made. Free tea and coffee is attracting all kinds of new customers and we badly need the traffic to keep our libraries open.'

'You won't hear me arguing with that,' Eliza replied, making herself a brew in a plastic cup. 'I was wondering, would it be okay to use one of the computers too? There's something I want to check, except I don't have any money to pay the user fee. I know it's only a couple of dollars, but do you mind if I pop back another day to sort you out?'

'Go for it. It's quiet today. Nobody on them. Use one for as long as you like. Anything I can help with?'

'I'm not sure. I'd like to find a lawyer, preferably one happy to work on a pro bono basis, who can assist me with a banking issue.'

'You could start with the ombudsman. They offer free advice to customers who have an issue with a financial services provider. I've never used them myself, but I've heard about them.'

'Ombudsman. Never heard of them, but thanks.'

Eliza headed to the bank of computers and logged on to Google. Her boys had taught her how to Internet search a long time ago, and although she had never invested in her own home computer, she knew how to navigate around with a few clicks of a mouse.

She ran a search and found what she was looking for instantly: FOS – Financial Ombudsman Service.

The pages were packed with information about how to lodge a dispute relating to financial organisations.

Eliza typed up a statement, outlining the information relating to her conversations with the bank and the charges deducted, and formally registered a complaint against her bank.

Next, she emailed her bank, sending them a copy of the same statement, with a note advising them she had taken up matters with the Financial Ombudsman Service.

'Doreen, do you have a phone I can use? It's a quick call to Clint, but it's in Japan. I'll ask him to call me straight back on your number. I'm so sorry to have to make so many unusual requests.'

'Don't apologise. How long have you been coming here? Twenty, twenty-five years? I'm your friend, Eliza. Call him and take as long as you need.' Doreen handed over her mobile phone.

Eliza phoned Clint and got him to call her straight back. Once she had explained the situation, she asked him for a small loan to tide her over for a few days. 'I'm so embarrassed to have to come to you about this.'

'Don't be daft, Mum. I'll wire you money right now into your account, but why did you not ask me to loan you the twenty per cent deposit in the first place?' he chided.

'You've got your own life and you don't need my burdens on your shoulders. Plus, it never occurred to me I'd get into this kind of a mess,' Eliza replied.

'Mum, you know I can afford to help you. How can the bank do something like this?'

'Don't get worked up about it, Clint. I'm dealing with things and I will not let them get away with putting me into debt like this.'

'Good on you, Mum. Now go home to your new place and relax.'

Eliza thanked him and hung up.

'Thank you, Doreen. For everything today.'

'Are you going to be okay?' Doreen asked.

'Absolutely,' Eliza replied. 'Everything is going to be just fine in no time at all.'

*

No time at all took nine months. It had been an awful period. Endless hours spent writing more letters, documenting everything she could remember about her conversations with Mr Garrity. She had provided a copy of her mortgage contract, which she had scoured end to end, reading every word to find reference to the insurance repayment. Nothing. No mention of the fee being taken back in one lump sum on property settlement day. The ombudsman asked for copies of her bank statements, showing her funds before the transaction, the immediate debt afterwards, and the ongoing debts she had been juggling, saved only by the ongoing payments her two boys were sending her. What angels they were to pay the removal men for her, and other bills to keep her lights switched on and food in her fridge.

Nine months! Longer than the time it took to grow her boys in her belly. Then the letter arrived from the ombudsman. Three reads it took. One where the words blurred. The second where she stopped so many times to wipe her eyes with a tissue that it became impossible to understand anything. Then the third read,

> Congratulations.
>
> We are delighted to tell you, Mrs Corbitt, that your claim has reached a conclusion and the investigation has been resolved in your favour.
>
> Please find a check from your bank of the full amount of your mortgage insurance, plus interest…

Eliza held the check to her chest. It was a relief to finally have closure on what had been a stressful situation to deal with. She phoned both her boys and told them she could finally pay them back everything she had borrowed.

'Nonsense,' they had scoffed. 'There's nothing to repay, Mum. It's our time to look after you whenever we can.'

Eliza had to sit down and make a cup of tea after that. She sipped it slowly, savouring the taste and sending prayers up to Bobby, thanking him for having a quiet word with the powers-that-be up there to help her out of a tight spot. He'd never left her. That she knew.

When she'd finished her tea, she picked up the morning newspaper, and flipped to the back section to find her horoscope. She loved reading what the stars were going to bring. Before she could find the page she was looking for, a headline jumped out and caught her eye.

Bank Shares Plummet

The article was reporting a situation surrounding her bank. It seemed thousands of customers had made claims against the bank relating to unfair bank charges.

Eliza read the article again, then she phoned Clint. 'How would you feel if I said I was thinking about spending my whole cheque in one go?' Eliza asked him.

'Are you mad?' Clint replied.

'No. In fact, I think I have just come up with the biggest brainwave of my entire life.'

'What brainwave?'

'I want to buy shares in the bank. Lots of shares. A whole ombudsman cheque's worth, in fact.'

Clint laughed.

Then Eliza laughed. Harder than she had ever laughed before.

It was quite a hysterical moment, but then the line went silent, just for a few moments.

'Do it, Mum. Do it.'

'I'll have to go to the library to find someone on the stock exchange who can sell me shares. I don't have a computer.'

They laughed again and then Eliza headed off to the library. It wasn't quite as nice as the one next to the old house. It had the same vast array of books, but no free hot drinks machine, and nobody as knowledgeable as Doreen about who to look up on the Internet.

Eliza clicked on the mouse and ran a search. Before closing time, she had bought all the shares she could at a rock-bottom price.

Tomorrow, she would read her horoscope and also read the business review section of the newspaper to watch how her shares were performing.

*

The day she sold her shares was one filled with celebrations that took her out of her wonderful little apartment. Eliza went to her new favourite tea shop on the foreshore with a view of the fabulously long Busselton jetty, the longest in the Southern Hemisphere. It was her favourite place to relax, watching the small red train drive passengers along the jetty to the tiny observation centre out in the ocean, then bring them back again. The passengers always seemed to be smiling. Windswept hair sometimes and rosy cheeks, but always smiling. The views in this part of the world were simply breathtaking. Stunning clear ocean lapping onto the whitest of sand. The water seemed so clear you would surely be able to see a shark approach from a mile away.

When her teacup, a lovely bone china teacup covered in pink roses, was empty, she went to the supermarket and bought all the ingredients she needed to make her favourite dinner of beef fillet. It had been one of the things she had in common with Bobby. Their love of a good medium-rare steak. Shopping bag in hand, she made her final stop before going home again. The bank.

'I'd like to see a mortgage advisor, please,' Eliza asked, when she reached the front of the queue.'

'Of course. Take a seat.' The teller pointed to some very peculiar-shaped armchairs in an array of bright colours. 'Can you confirm your name?'

Eliza gave her some basic information and sat down on the edge of the purple one that had a curved arm on one side and no arm on the other. Modern furnishings were not a patch on her comfortable old sofa. Luckily, she didn't have long to wait before the teller reappeared.

'Mrs Corbitt, I can show you through now to see Mr Garrity.'

'Mr Garrity?'

'Yes, he transferred here a few months ago. He's our mortgage advisor. Is there a problem?'

Eliza chuckled. 'No problem. That would be great if you could show me through, thanks.'

She followed the teller through the branch to a frosted-glass meeting room, and then left her in the open doorway.

'Mrs Corbitt, come in.' Mr Garrity stood and offered his hand.

Eliza shook it. Weak, she thought. Bobby always had such a firm handshake.

'Erm, would you like to take a seat.'

Eliza sat down, marvelling at the interesting shade of beetroot that Mr Garrity's cheeks seemed to be turning. 'I'll keep it brief, shall I? I'm sure you're awfully busy.'

'No, no. I don't have another appointment for another hour or so. Take your time to talk through the problem.'

'Problem? Oh, there's no problem. Whatever gave you that idea?'

'Oh…I'm erm, well, I thought…'

'I'm here to pay off my mortgage.' Eliza smiled at Mr Garrity.

'Pay it off?'

'Yes. In full.'

'In full?'

'Yes. Would you like my bank card?' Eliza reached into her handbag and pulled out her lovely tan leather purse that Bobby had bought her as a Christmas gift a few months before he passed away. She slid her bank card over the desk between them. 'The funds are all in the account that you deducted that huge mortgage insurance fee from way back. It's all there. More than enough to pay off the full amount of the mortgage. I hate debt. Isn't it just a dreadful position to be in?'

Mr Garrity took a look at the card and tapped her details into his keyboard. 'Wow. I see a very large sum of money was credited into your account today.'

'Yes, very large indeed. I sold all my shares. Amazing what a good investment can yield.'

'It certainly is. Everything seems in order, Mrs Corbitt. I'll need to go through the early mortgage repayment fees with you. There's a small fee needed to get out of your mortgage early, applicable when you pay back the total amount owed on your mortgage.'

'I believe that there is more than enough in my account to cover the small fee, and to leave me with a nice little nest egg in there too. However, you do understand if I ask for another person in the bank to provide details of this fee, fully outlined, in writing, for me to read and sign my consent.'

'Of course. Everything we do in the bank is put in writing to make sure there is no ambiguity around our fees. It's best practice to make sure everything is transparent in our transactions with our valued customers.'

'Well, isn't that just an amazing piece of news.' Eliza stood and offered her hand.

Mr Garrity shook it. 'Before you leave, Mrs Corbitt, would you find it awfully intrusive of me to ask what shares you invested in?'

'The bank.'

'Pardon?'

'I bought and sold shares in the bank. Stroke of luck that I bought at just the right moment, right when a whole tort of customers seemed to be winning cases of unfair fees being charged and the bank share price hit rock bottom. So glad the stocks recovered in such a marvellous manner. Must be all those best practices put in place.'

Eliza swept out of the bank and went home to her apartment, where she made herself a nice cup of tea.

A Dog's Life

Waves crash, thunderous like my mood. Churning up sand and washing broken shells along the shore of Windynook Bay outside my window. Kitesurfers pepper the sky, bright speckles of colour defying gravity. This stretch of coast is a haven for water sports fanatics. It benefits from erratic weather, everything from searing heatwaves to earth-shattering storms, often all in one day. Creates the best swell for miles around. Whenever I come back here, the wave of nostalgia is intense, like I'm surfing through one of those tunnels and might not make it out the other side.

I pull the floral curtains closed to block out the morning sun and lie back on the double bed, hands locked behind my head. The cool, white Egyptian cotton sheets are rumpled and full of crumbs from the room service delivery of hot buttery croissants and sticky pastries. What with having a lie in, it was too late to squeeze in bacon and eggs in the communal dining room downstairs. Thankfully, the ancient owners offered to bring up baked goods since I'm a returning guest. Excellent service for a local bed and breakfast. Must give them a five-star rating.

The fan whirrs above my head, wobbling as it goes. Hopefully it doesn't bring the ceiling down on my dark mop of hair. That would drop my online review to at least three stars. It stresses me out, whizzing around and around, forever stuck in groundhog day. I'm unable to break free of a vicious cycle too. A goddamn gerbil on a wheel going nowhere. Screwing my eyes closed replaces the fan with an image of Nadine on the back of my eyelids.

I miss her like crazy. The touch of her soft skin is forever imprinted in my mind, as sharp as this morning's black coffee that washed down breakfast in bed. Her shoulder-length chestnut hair spread over the feather pillow, tousled and velvet to the touch. Even though she's not here now, I can recall her intoxicating smell. Clean with a faint hint of lavender from the miniature bottles in the bed and breakfast bathroom.

The void of her being gone hurts. She has to work. Don't we all. Me in the garage out of town, my rough mechanic hands always dirty with a pungent smell of oil (might steal whatever is left of the lavender goods on check out). Nadine has dry hands too, from spending so many hours at the salon, scrubbing tatty pooches behind the ears and clipping their nails. Managing the Pooch Parlour was always her destiny. She'll inherit the McGuire's Veterinary Clinic too when her folks pass away. Animal mad, she is. Think she loves dogs more than she loves humans. There is nothing on earth I love more than her. Not even close. I love her so much it hurts to breathe.

*

From our first day of high school, when my seat in geography class was positioned behind hers, I knew we were destined to be together.

'Matthew Briggs! I asked you a question,' the teacher hollered.

I was slouched, elbows on the desk, tired after suffering another bout of insomnia the night before. Can never seem to manage a decent sleep. The teacher got me sitting upright. 'Sorry, miss. Could you repeat the question?'

'I should not have to…'

The right hand belonging to the girl in front flew up into the air.

'Yes, Nadine?' the teacher asked.

Nadine gave a very informative answer about the problem litter was causing the environment, especially in Western Australia, where plastic bags were getting washed up on some of the beaches in our surrounding area.

Nadine couldn't see the grin on my face. Nobody had ever saved me from a humiliating rant from a teacher before.

During recess, I saw her in the corridor shoving an English literature textbook into her locker, so I sauntered over, hands tucked in pockets. 'Thanks.'

'For what?'

'Dunno,' I shrugged.

Nadine shut the locker with a bang and wandered off.

I stood there, watching the way her ponytail bounced on the top of her head, wanting to kick myself black and blue for not finding some flowery words to start a decent conversation.

But after that, she started throwing me a nod whenever we passed in the hallway at school. About a year later, in science one day, she partnered with me to dissect a frog. Her hand touched mine as we lay the frog on its back and spread its miniature limbs as wide as we could. Nadine's lip quivered as I used the scalpel to make an incision. Think she realised right then I was a tough guy. It was the best day of my life.

We cycled home together after the last bell that day, me tucked in behind Nadine. My ancient bike kept pace with her newer wheels as we headed towards the suburb where we both used to live back then. Nothing but fate could have placed us a couple of streets apart from one another in a country the size of Australia.

'Wanna take a detour to the beach?' I called to her.

She silently swerved to take a left-hand turn towards the sandy cove at the far end of Windynook Bay.

I pedalled hard, sweat dripping from my forehead as I pushed to keep up with her. We went faster and faster, up kerbs, down pathways and through the shaded archway created by ancient trees. A scattering of fallen cones crackled under my tyres.

The foreshore was busy around Carley's Café. The place made a killing selling every possible flavour of milkshake and soft, whipped gelato.

We got to the car park quickly and hopped off the bikes, slotting them into the metal rack. Nadine pulled off her helmet. I wasn't wearing one. Mum would never have wasted money on something so trivial. After Dad walked out not long after my seventh birthday, she struggled to make the bills, so I didn't mind. It was way too hot to wear one anyway.

Nadine had a bike lock which she wrapped around both our front wheels. She could have skipped mine. Nobody would bother stealing my rust bucket.

'Nice bike, by the way,' I said.

'Thanks. I got it for Christmas.'

'I figured.'

'Do you want to swim?'

I badly wanted to take a dip. The water looked calm and flat, an endless glistening paradise. It was impossible not to feel the tug of a swim after our hot and sweaty cycle.

'I've no boardies.'

'Swim in those.' Nadine nodded at my school uniform of grey shorts and a white shirt.

'What about you?'

'It's cool.' Nadine kicked off her shoes then stripped off her green and white striped school dress, throwing it over the handlebars of her bike. Underneath, she was wearing black tight gym shorts and a black sports bra. It wasn't the first time I had discreetly stared at her figure, but it was the first time I'd seen her so exposed. My cheeks grew flushed. She was so beautiful, with small but perfectly formed breasts, and long, tanned limbs.

She started jogging over the sand. 'Let's go!'

I tugged off my scuffed black lace-ups and left them beside the bikes. One of my shoes had a hole in the bottom, so I made sure I placed the sole flat to the ground, so it wasn't noticeable. We laughed as we ran over the sand, jumping over pieces of washed-up seaweed. Parents helping their toddlers to build sandcastles were scattered along the beach. We passed all the happy families and headed to the farthest end of the beach where it was deserted. A sandbank blocked out the road behind us and a pile of enormous rocks was to the far side, so we were completely sheltered. We clambered across them and sat on the biggest boulder which jutted out over a rock pool. My breath was uneven, panting with the exertion of the run and the intense midday heat that crept in. There was silence between us, but I didn't mind. It was pleasant listening to the sound of the waves lap against the shore.

There were a couple of kids paddling around on bodyboards a little way off, but no hardcore surfers around. Most tended to head up to Trigg or all the way down to Yallingup, where the breezy conditions and stronger currents created a far better swell for Western Australian daredevils. Here, the outlying reef made for calmer conditions.

'Shark!' Nadine shouted, pointing towards the horizon.

'Where?' I leapt to my bare feet, holding my hand over my eyes to shade them as I scoured the water for a fin.

'Gotcha,' she laughed.

I gave her a gentle shove which made her slip into the shallow rock pool. 'Idiot.'

'I had you, though. You should have seen the shock on your face. It was so cool.'

'One of these days I'll get you back.'

'Whatever. Are you coming in?'

I pulled off my white school shirt and threw it onto the rocks, then she splashed me. I felt way to skinny and was acutely aware of my tiny biceps. It was right then I decided to get a job as fast as I could, to make enough money to go to gym and sort myself out with a six-pack.

I lowered myself in until the water reached my shins, then bent to give the pool a swirl with my hands. It sent ripples around Nadine, who lay down to submerge her whole body. She tugged at my leg and I toppled onto my knees, the water soaking the bottom of my shorts.

The water was icy, but I lay down next to Nadine and dunked my whole head under for a moment to get the initial chill over in one go.

When I emerged, Nadine had fully submerged herself too. She pushed her wet hair off her forehead. Drips of water ran down her face and neck as she sat up, her leg touching mine underwater.

I threw her a shy smile.

'What?' she asked.

'Nothing.' I moved slowly, afraid she might bolt at any sudden movement, but she was frozen to the spot. The space between us closed and my breath caught in my throat. The kiss was quick, a sloppy peck on the cheek and I pulled back fast.

Nadine's eyebrows were furrowed.

Panic rumbled in my gut. 'Sorry.'

'Why are you sorry?'

'Dunno. Why are you frowning?'

'Why did you stop?'

I shrugged and she leaned forward to kiss me again, pecking me fully on the lips. It was nice. Wet and soft. I was determined to part my lips next time like Mum did with Dad when I was younger, way before he ran off into the abyss with that other stupid lady from his work.

*

I stretch before I fall into a deep slumber and plump the pillow to prop myself up comfortably. It wouldn't do to sleep too late. I'm thankful to be enjoying a day off. Everyone needs a day of rest from the monotony sometimes, but I don't want to waste it counting sheep.

My limbs ache from constant training. Running up and down the hilly beach paths, phone strapped around the right biceps. The arm muscles have been expanding every day. Fittest I've ever been. Can't say I'm particularly vain, but I want to look good for her. Nadine has never been high maintenance about her own appearance. It's one of the things that attracted me to her in the first place. A natural look that suits her perfectly. Sometimes a hint of mascara, but that's it. Always had a complex about her eyelashes being shorter than the average girl, but otherwise she's confident in how she looks. When I look at her, I want her to stare back with wonderment, mirroring the intensity of how I drink her in. I don't want those eyelashes of hers to blink. Not even for a second.

Room service disturbs me with a knock on the door. Don't even get a chance to cover my naked body before the maid waltzes in with a pile of fluffy white towels. Gets more than she bargained for, seeing me lying here in all my glory. Judging by the burning colour spreading up her cheeks, she's way more embarrassed than me. Pretty little blonde thing; perky, but not my type. Really is frustrating to wake up without Nadine here, though. Despite the fatigue my body feels, every muscle needs another workout to blow off the pent-up frustration I feel with not having her constantly at my side. I've become so much stronger from applying discipline when pumping iron. That's the secret to success in life. Unwavering commitment. I should write one of those self-help books to share my wisdom with the world. So many fun names I could call it. Something about discipline with a four-letter curse in the title would hit the mark.

I'll head off soon for a fitness session. Do an hour of cardio, row to nowhere and break into a sweat while skiing on the machine with built-in TV. The gym should be quiet so no doubt I will get way more done. No distractions from annoying lithe whippets wearing Lycra second skins. Nadine has curves. Not overly so, but in all the right places. One of her greatest assets is she doesn't flaunt any of her other amazing physical assets. She hides her perfection under a plaid shirt and jeans. It will make peeling them off all the more exciting. I know what's under there. The smoothest skin and that mole on the inside of her right thigh. Running my thumb over that dark little spot is what I focus on when I'm bored at work. When I'm having a bad day tinkering with a motor that's rusty as hell and needs a defibrillator to get it going again. Without the distraction of that mole, I would have thrown in the oil-soaked rag a long time ago. I'm going to have her tonight. Every soft inch of her will quiver under my touch, giving her what she needs before I take my pleasure. That's what relationships are about. Giving and taking.

*

The stiff jog uphill is tough on the lungs, despite my fitness level. I'm relieved to come down the other side again, towards Carley's Café. The tables and chairs on the pavement are full of ladies brunching, the kind who pack off their husbands to work their fingers to the bone in the city and then complain to their friends about not receiving enough attention at home. As I level with the very last table, I spot Briana and Harley sipping coffee, a couple I recognise as friends of Nadine's. They work with her at the dog grooming salon and spend half their day walking the pooches around town. There's no sign of Nadine, but her instantly recognisable two huskies, Milo and Zena, are curled up underneath the table. Nadine is obsessed with this four-legged pair she's had since pups. Abby and Harley are much the same.

My heart pounds as Abby picks up her mobile phone. Shade covers my forehead frown as I tug my black sports cap down and break into a sprint. Cyclists whizz past on the bike path and I do my utmost to chase them. The track runs for several kilometres, winding past the dunes on one side that mark the spot I first kissed Nadine. Windynook Bay haunts like the Seaside Bar and Grill are on the other side.

At the top of the final killer hill stretch of my run is a vantage point. Nobody is around as I sit on the wooden bench and stare out at the waves crashing below. A couple of jumpers have taken their own lives here. Easy to see why this spot holds appeal for taking the last couple of breaths before checking out. It's stunning. Treacherous, rugged rocks rise from the water. You wouldn't stand a chance.

Nadine and I once made out here, years ago. A few months after that first kiss at the beach. Horny, panting teenagers, our tongues exploring each other, bodies pressed tight. If she had wanted to take a leap of faith back then, I would have held her hand and gone over the edge with her.

Thinking of Nadine, I decide against gym. It can wait. I get back to my feet and loop back the way I came. Briana and Harley have gone, thank goodness. Neither are people I want to see right now. They are so tight with Nadine, they were always jealous of our time together as a couple. Our relationship is impossible to understand. It's the kind of adoration that consumes time. Fills my dreams at night and swallows me whole during the day.

I run faster and faster towards the Pooch Parlour, slowing down on the final approach to the building. The building has been modernised, with a wooden enclosure out back enclosing the dustbins so they are not an eyesore. I wait next to the bins catching my breath. Nadine sometimes comes out to toss away black bin liners full to the brim of dog hair she's shaved off in her never-ending grooming sessions, but there's no sign of her so I move out and creep across the garden to peek in the window, looking into the galley kitchen. Nadine has her back to me as she pours boiling water from the red kettle to make a cup of tea in a polka dot mug with the chipped handle. Her hair is pulled back in a ponytail. The nape of her neck is long and beautiful. It's an erogenous zone. Amazing how a woman can quiver when you run a finger around the hairline, light as a feather.

My hand closes around the handle to the back door, turning the knob slowly so it doesn't creak and give away the element of surprise. Last thing I want is to set any dogs in there off too. Barking mad, some of her furry customers are. The door opens an inch, just enough to see she still has her back to me. The rush is incredible, pumping blood to all the parts of my body that make me feel alive.

I shove the door with my shoulder and barge in, grabbing Nadine from behind. The scream is a delight. A teaspoon clatters to the floor, slipping from her grasp. She tries to bite my hand as I put my palm firmly over her plump pink lips. Rough is good. I pull her in to me, our bodies fusing as one, holding her for long enough for her to smell me. The lavender scent from my morning shower lingers on my skin as it was on hers that day all those years ago when we shared a bed in the Windynook Bay Bed and Breakfast. How I craved her this morning as I ate those crumbling pastries alone and reminisced.

It takes all my strength to pull her towards the open door. There is a perfect spot outside for making love, behind the bush in the corner of the back garden. She wriggles and I laugh in her ear, knowing how much this fine woman always liked to play games. It's payback time for the way she gave me a bone then made me play chase for years.

Before we make it to the dense green bush, Nadine trips and I fall on top of her. The thrill of the tussle is too much to handle. No time to wait. My weight keeps her pinned down as I tug at her jeans, desperate for skin against skin.

The growl from deep within Nadine is guttural. It's there again, louder this time. It's not from her. It's from behind. The bite to my ankle hurts. Breaks through and draws blood. I twist my head just enough to catch a glimpse of both huskies attacking me. I kick out, making one yelp. A tall silhouette is looming in the doorway. Could be Harley. Saw me on the run and came straight here to warn Nadine. Interfering idiot.

Nadine wriggles out from under me as the man moves from the house and grabs me in an arm lock. It's not Harley. It's the police.

The regret of not being able to finish what I've started is overwhelming.

'I'm sorry, Nadine. I…I…love you."

The slap across my face from her is unexpected. It's sobering.

All the frustration of pining for Nadine since we broke up a few years ago spills out in a torrent of tears. Watching her from afar has been torture since the injunction was issued. She accused me of stalking her, but what was I supposed to do when she refused to take my calls and blocked my profile on social media? She was single. Still is. That's what makes everything so confusing. This whole situation is hell.

I can't accept her moving on.

It will never be over.

It's a dog's life.

Bleach

'The usual?' Leeroy asks.

'Please.'

I tap my phone to pay for the coffee. The evolution of technology is incredible. It's a privilege to work in the industry, developing the latest widgets for a global giant. It's a riot being the only woman on the executive board, constantly swimming upstream against the status quo.

My favourite chair is empty. Unusual as this place usually gets decent traffic. Best free-trade beans in town. I head straight for the patterned armchair. Comfortable, with contours that have moulded around a thousand bodies. There's a new tear just behind my neck and stuffing is already spilling out. Ticklish on the skin just beneath my cropped blonde hair.

As I wait for Leeroy to froth my morning brew, I check out the latest graffiti decorating the walls of the laneway café. There's a new floor-to-ceiling piece up. An indigenous man with long dreadlocks, playing the digeridoo. An empty cup is positioned at his bare, dirty, feet and an intricate cerise pink TAG has been sprayed beneath the mural. Impossible not to recognise the street artist. One of Australia's finest by the name of Bleach. The culprit has a reputation for depicting social injustice images in their designs that spectacularly pop up overnight. They're so good, nobody seems to care if they are illegal vandalism or commissioned requests. The consensus is they generate conversation about the taboo. Challenging the world through experimental visuals displayed in the public domain. For years, the paparazzi have been unsuccessful in shining sunlight on the identity of the person responsible for these unique paintings decorating the cities' otherwise bland brickwork. All they've managed to report is Bleach sprays an ever-changing colourful canvas that is visible one day and cleaned away by the council the next. Shame this masterpiece will be scrubbed off by tomorrow.

'Extra hot today,' Leeroy says, winking as he passes my cappuccino over. 'Bet someone tech savvy posted on Insta already. Amazing control of the can.'

'Sure is.' I raise my cup in salute. He's the only person who knows what I do after dark.

'I gotta share some sad news with you, given you're my best customer and all,' Leeroy says.

'Oh?'

'They're shutting me down. Landlord says development plans he lodged to gentrify the place have been approved. The whole building is getting a facelift. Time for a modern minimalist look is what he said. Something about wanting to create a cultural hub for tourism.'

'But this is where the urban pulse is at. Don't they get it?'

Leeroy shakes his head and goes back to his barista station.

I take a sip of my coffee. Burns my tongue. I intend to flip this thing. Use my tongue to burn the powers that be on these decisions. Give them a scathing piece of my mind.

I scan the walls. Hope someone listens, otherwise next time I see them, they won't just be cleaned. They'll be whitewashed.

Just like the conforming brain.

Rolling in the Mud

The grumble of my stomach is loud, echoing my desperation for a muffin to satisfy my sweet tooth. I consider taking one before the platter gets whisked away from the boardroom to the kitchen, but the seagulls are out there, squawking for crumbs to devour in their rostered tea break. I'd prefer they enjoy the baked goods rather than me. It's unfair the executive board can order catering on credit when there aren't even vending machines on the floors for keeping the flocks satisfied.

'No thanks.' I give Bernadette a warm smile as she offers them round.

Bernadette is the new executive assistant who came in through the back door to work for the CEO, Marcus, only a week ago. Marcus hired her after she was recommended by his mother-in-law, who knew her from book club. My guess is she's nearing retirement age, but the combination of a smooth forehead and a wrinkled neck makes it difficult to tell. Maybe she injects Botox, but who cares? These days, half the population is shooting a foreign substance into their system. Whatever her beauty regime, Bernadette looks amazing. She easily carries off the bright red lipstick, and that beige pencil skirt is a perfect second skin. The only way I'll come close to fitting into a pencil skirt is by sticking to my principles and feeding the birds.

'Who's up next?' Marcus asks, his hand hovering over a wireless mouse that is the shape of a novelty yellow Ferrari. Bernadette should be manoeuvring the PowerPoint decks on his behalf, but she's just disappeared. Not that it matters. In my dealings with her, she barely seems to know how to use a computer. Although technology innovation may have passed her by, she's shown an uncanny ability to locate misplaced files, and can negotiate the best deal from the toughest stationery suppliers.

'Juanita,' Jack says, grabbing the laser pointer from the polished, tinted-glass boardroom table.

He's wrong. The agenda says he's up next, but I bite my tongue as Marcus taps the bonnet of the Ferrari and closes the last presentation. He manoeuvres PowerPoint to my opening slide. It's a black and white portrait of our office amidst Perth's skyscrapers, captioned with an oversized font screaming,

JUANITA SWANEPOEL
CORPORATE LIAISON DIRECTOR
TALENT CAPITAL MANAGEMENT AND DIVERSITY

Next time, I'll omit my name and title from my slides. I shouldn't bother conforming with the cookie-cutter introduction used by the rest of the executive board. It's done just to be sure we don't forget who we are. The pretentious title was allocated when I transferred to Western Australia from the Cape Town office. It's posh corporate jargon for human resources. In a nutshell, though, my job is simple. The global bigwigs transferred me to Australia to make an impact on employee utilisation through reducing excessive sick leave by poking people with a flu shot. They are also counting on me to avoid legal action minefields relating to unfair dismissal claims. There's so much workforce churn in online retail that intake standards have been lowered to embark on manic recruitment campaigns.

Historically, we've been prone to hiring substandard performers who ultimately end up getting fired. Since accepting the position here, I'm ashamed to admit that embedding diversity initiatives and much-needed quotas to balance the gender inequity hasn't happened as quickly as I'd have liked. It's been a juggernaut effort merely keeping the cupboard replenished. I intend to correct this as soon as I get a chance to reprioritise. As an established global retail firm, we should be a magnet for attracting the best people from the market, but there are giants who trod players like us into the pavement next to the chewed-up gum. We're not a Fortune 500 investor's dream. We manage to stay afloat from maintaining decent trading levels within the half-dozen countries we operate in, but the likes of eBay and Amazon have the lion's share of consumer monopoly profits, as well as brawny household name brands to entice new blood. To compete, we minions sell our grannies to the devil for a discounted price, with next-day delivery and free postage with bubble-wrap packaging thrown in.

Jack hands me the laser pointer for the projector.

'Thanks,' I say.

The churlish men take great delight in hiding the laser pointer in random places, but Bernadette found it this morning in the storeroom next to the toilet rolls. She knows from last week's meeting I'm the only one who bothers using it. Everyone else relies on Marcus to change slides but it seems like poor use of CEO skills to me. He should be concocting strategies for achieving better top-line growth and maximising bottom-line return. I press the pointer, searching for the red beam that if aimed at someone's head marks them for assassination. It's nowhere to be found, which is a shame. There are one or two heads in here I'd like to blast off!

My name remains fixed on the enormous white screen that would have most cinemas eating their hearts out. I flip open the battery compartment of the laser pointer. It's empty.

Bernadette, who has just walked back in minus the muffins, says, 'That's weird, Juanita. I checked earlier and it definitely had batteries. Should I nip to my desk and get a pack of Duracell?'

Jack reclines in his black leather chair and smirks as he stares out the window at the view of high-rise steel and glass corporate offices, interspersed with glimpses of the Swan River.

'Women,' mutters Larry, the principal officer of strategic sales. 'Can't we get a move on? Forget all this talk of batteries. It's making us fall behind.'

I bite my tongue. We're already three hours behind schedule due to his earlier waffling, where he painfully dissected the lowlights of every client lost this century, instead of talking about the highlights of his top ten immediate prospects.

'Don't worry,' I tell Bernadette. 'I'm sure Marcus doesn't mind driving a while longer.'

She gives me a knowing look, cementing the sisterhood bond growing between us. I'll make it my mission to train her. With a little coaching and mentoring, Bernadette will be employee of the month in no time. She takes a seat at the right-hand side of Marcus, and sucks on a straw dipped in a clear cup with dome-shaped lid. The green sludge contents look positively radioactive. I really should try to take a leaf out of Bernadette's book and swap coffee for a healthy smoothie. Although I know the subject matter of my presentation inside out, I'm on edge from an overdose of caffeine.

Marcus clicks the Ferrari. Virtual curtains close across my slide and slowly reopen with a swish and sway, revealing the new incentive plan that is destined to leave everyone with a poisonous taste in their mouth like they've licked lead paint. Marcus must have fucked with my presentation. I'm a minimalist. No milk in my coffee. French-manicured nails. An apartment painted white, containing a white leather couch with matching white scatter cushions. I always have my slides progress in a clean, no-nonsense fashion. There's no ripple or honeycomb, no fade in or out, no goddamn curtains!

I doubt the culprit is Bernadette. She would likely be more comfortable changing a typewriter ribbon than adjusting PowerPoint transitions. My eyes scan the Caucasian males in their suits, seated around the boardroom table. Their pinstripes blur into barcodes on a conveyer belt. Larry seems preoccupied with stuffing a blueberry muffin in his mouth when he thinks nobody is looking. Charlie, the pompous head of distribution, is browsing his Blackberry. When the latest iPhones were rolled out in a new internal telecommunications deal, he refused to switch to an Apple device. He hit average retirement age some time before the first Aboriginal Australians formed their strong spiritual connection with this wonderful land, so with any luck he'll drive off into the sunset on his golf buggy soon and we can terminate the special Blackberry contract we have in place for him.

At the top of the table is the CFO, Bruce, who has flown in from Sydney to preside over us, but he is fast asleep.

Jack Barbarella is the only one looking my way, his piercing blue eyes causing sweat to pool under my arms like I'm stockpiling for Mundaring Weir. Jack, the vice president of global trends and future transformation, always gets me riled. Making my neck turn red is the only thing he can predict with any certainty.

'I see you've opened with a diversity slide,' he says. A smirk decorates his craggy white face, showing off the veneers I assume he installed on interest-free credit, since nobody got paid a dime out of last year's bonus allocation.

Our targets were destined for failure after a one-off cheap Black Friday marketing campaign was hit by a viral outbreak of clones across Australia. Competitor price wars remained problematic for eleven months, sinking retail spend to an all-time low.

No shit, Sherlock, I want to hiss, but my business coach, assigned as part of our mindfulness and personal development programme, has been drilling a phrase into me over the last ten sessions: 'If you roll in the mud with a pig you'll get dirty.'

I smile at Jack. 'Correct.'

'And how are we doing with attracting another much-needed female leader to the board to balance our business dynamics?' he asks.

'We've held interviews with several very talented females to improve the ratios in leadership roles and on our own succession plans. It's a shame none seemed of the calibre Marcus was looking for. Nevertheless, we won't give up. We've a mountain of work to do, as you can see.' My arm sweeps the room while Marcus progresses onto the next slide about our gender pay gap.

Jack gets up and wanders into my personal space to peer at the spreadsheet snapshot on the screen.

I glance towards Bruce for moral support on the financial numbers. He's still having forty winks, so I point to the column summarising salary comparisons. 'Let's start with…'

'Is there any truth to the rumour that we are paying thirty-eight per cent more for male executives than females?' Jack interrupts.

If you roll in the mud…

If you roll in the mud…

It takes every ounce of self-restraint to keep my anger at bay.

'Since I'm the only female on the board, I've not been privy to each of your salary packages. However, when we consider the average pay across all other employees, the company clearly has a gender pay problem. We need to reduce the remuneration discrepancy and we absolutely must continue to tackle the low percentage of female senior leaders in our organisation.'

'So, is it safe to say you haven't thoroughly researched in preparation for today? Since the sample data sets are not comprehensive, the pay gap you refer to may be entirely speculative.' Jack holds up his two index fingers and wiggles them as he utters the word 'speculative'.

I want to stick two different fingers up in response, but it wouldn't be polite. Instead, I say, 'The issue is very real and needs to be addressed.'

'In the interest of time, can I suggest we keep moving along?' Jack nods at Marcus.

I don't know if it's accidental or intentional, but Marcus seems to have hit one of the F keys, shrinking the visual image on the screen to an unreadable size.

'Oops, sorry, Juanita.' He clicks the Ferrari with such ferocity I fear he may spark a fire in the engine.

The hands of the clock on the far wall tick, announcing we are so far off schedule it will be yet another late night at the office. My own hands feel like useless spare parts, dangling lifelessly by my sides. I consciously raise one to tuck an unruly strand of auburn hair that's escaped from my sculptured bun behind my ear. A few weeks ago, Marcus instructed the entire executive board to attend an online webinar on body language for billionaires. Ever since, I've been cognisant of every tiny movement I make.

'We are the Champions' suddenly blares from beneath the charcoal carpet tiles, where there is a discreetly hidden state-of-the-art sound system. I'm told it was installed during the mining boom at a time when Australian shoppers didn't bother waiting for two-for-one deals before spending their hard-earned cash.

'Sorry, I've no idea how the music switched itself on,' Marcus apologises again. He reverses the Ferrari and the music cuts out.

Jack forms a gun with his hand and winks as he pulls the imaginary trigger at Marcus. 'Freddie Mercury. Nice.'

He's been brown-nosing Marcus since the Christmas party last month. Marcus drank too much eggnog and let it slip he was being considered for a transfer to the New York headquarters. Since then, speculation that one of the current executives would be promoted into the Australian CEO role has been spreading through the office like a bushfire. On her second day in the job, Bernadette confided in me that she caught the payroll team running a sweepstake and Jack was the front-runner.

My slide zooms into focus, revealing female retention issues, lack of flexible hours, the need for a paternity leave policy, the mess over maternity leave accruals, funding constraints for the diversity council, and complaints about overspending on eggnog. As I reel it all off, I bitterly regret not having that energy-booster muffin. There's nothing in my segment about profit and loss, or mergers and acquisitions, so it's understandable Bruce suddenly lets out a thunderous snore. I forgive him on the basis he's clocked up a lot of air miles just to be here.

Jack lives a ten-minute walk from the CBD and doesn't even attempt to stifle a yawn. A poster behind his head, of a yacht anchored off Rottnest Island with the slogan 'Success is a journey, not a destination' printed on its starboard side, catches my eye. The curtains close and open, presenting half-a-dozen old boys' club bullying and harassment accusations lodged in the last month. With another swish, they unleash confidential information about a mutiny, led by an intern, that has been snowballing in clandestine meetings around the photocopier. All because his request for a carbonated-water cooler on the eighteenth floor was declined by procurement.

'The amount of time we've spent on this water cooler saga is a joke,' Jack says. 'Just buy it for the damn intern.'

'We can't,' I reply. 'If we install one on the eighteenth, we'll be obliged to roll them out on all fifty levels. Even if procurement did approve, finance will overrule, exactly like they did with the vending machine request.'

The Sydney purse strings, Bruce, makes us all jump as he suddenly sits up. 'Juanita is right. It will affect the forecast.'

'Take it from my budget,' Jack offers.

My Harvard-educated business coach will be furious, but I can't resist correcting him. 'That's very noble of you, Jack, but you don't have a budget.'

'Are you saying I'm nothing but an expense centre? What kind of demoralising remark is that for someone who brings blood, sweat and tears to this business every day? Global trends and future transformation is of vital importance so we can predict what is down the line for us and plan accordingly.'

Jack straightens his paisley tie. I want to yank it tighter around his throat.

'I'm simply saying there is an affordability issue with the carbonated-water request, and right now, we've got a gender pay gap to sort out, diversity targets to improve on, and redundancy costs to fund. We would be better off putting our money there.'

Jack is so close to me I can see his nostrils flare as he glares at me. I return the stare, unblinking, until he begins pacing again with his thumbs hooked together behind his back. When he turns, his poker face has been pasted on. 'You, of all people, with your fairness and equity crusade, should know this is a human rights issue that needs to be taken up with finance. Someone asks for fizzy water instead of still, we've a legal obligation to provide it, you know, to accommodate diversity and all.'

I hold back a sigh. 'We're not breaching any legal rights.'

'So, you're a lawyer now, are you?'

'No, I'm simply...'

'Then we need to seek professional advice. Can we have it added to the executive action log that someone needs to place an investigative call with the Fair Work Commission?' Jack glares at Bernadette, who is close to finishing the last of her green sludge.

'Don't worry, Bernadette. I'll do it,' Marcus says, jotting a note on the lined pad in front of him. 'Who shall I assign it to?'

'Since our leader of talent capital management and diversity has not deemed it a priority to challenge the thinking on this water debacle, I'm happy to take it on for you, Marcus,' Jack offers.

Bruce is rubbing both eyes to wake himself up.

No doubt for the benefit of the CFO, Jack adds, 'To achieve the forecast, maybe we can make some cutbacks in Juanita's department. We can offset these savings against the water purchase. I'll write a return-on-investment business case. It's something I feel incredibly passionate about. We need to fight for the moral rights of our people if we are to maintain a positive culture in this organisation. These sorts of things can make or break a CEO.'

'About making or breaking a CEO, I'd like to hand over to Marcus to present my final slide.' I cross the room and sit next to Marcus. 'I can drive the Ferrari for you.'

Marcus pushes the mouse my way and stands. 'Well, erm, as some of you already know, I have been considering a position in the Big Apple, and I don't mean Apple as in iPhones.'

Everyone guffaws at this lame joke.

'Well, I've accepted a transfer. I'll be leaving Australia at the end of the month.'

Everyone rises to pump Marcus's hand and slap his back.

When the commotion subsides, he continues, 'Behind the scenes, there has been a lot of debate with the global capital talent management team in New York, who wanted to conduct both an internal and an external search for my replacement.'

Jack's mouth opens, catching flies. 'External search?'

'Yes, there were some valid points raised around making sure we appoint the best person to take over the board of Australia. However, I managed to dissuade them from considering external options in favour of looking at our current executives. I wasn't involved in the selection process, but just this morning, they confirmed they were promoting from within.'

Jack fiddles with his silver cufflinks. 'Thank goodness for that.'

'Juanita, could you bring up that last slide with this month's internal talent appointments?' asks Marcus.

I click the Ferrari. The last slide shows the black and white office portrait, captioned with an oversized font that screams,

JUANITA SWANEPOEL
CHIEF EXECUTIVE OFFICER

Rumbles ripple around the boardroom table. I get a nod from Bruce and what could be either a wink or a nervous twitch from Larry. Marcus sits again without tossing so much as a word of congratulations in my direction.

'Bernadette, later today, would you replace the batteries in the laser pointer and lock it away in my desk, thanks?' I ask her with a smile. 'I'll bring it to the next meeting to ensure everyone is equipped to drive their own slides.'

'Of course,' she replies.

'Let's keep rolling, shall we, Jack?' I say jovially. 'It's your turn to present and I'm so looking forward to your predictions about the future.'

Jack turns as green as Bernadette's smoothie dregs. I stand as he takes over the stage, my shoulders back and my head high. Beneath my heels, the mud is drying, forming a solid foundation to build on.

Acknowledgements

The writing of this book, much like life, has not been a clean run. The journey of scrubbing grit from beneath broken fingernails and wading through mud caking under tired feet has been exhausting but exhilarating. There are so many people along the way who have encouraged me to dig deep into exploring unforgiving territory where the dirtiest lies streak through the darkest truths. This is fiction after all.

Stephen Matthews and the professional crew at Ginninderra Press, thank you for having the vision to take my medley of contemporary short stories under your wing and for creating something so closely aligned with my own vision that we were always destined to be on the same page.

Clive Newman, thank you for constantly putting my imposter syndrome worries at ease and providing ongoing advice on my various writing projects. Your wisdom as a literary agent is invaluable and I would be lost in my navigations without you guiding me in the right direction.

Several of these short stories have also placed in literary competitions or previously appeared in international publications, with thanks to the following organisations: Inktears, Wolvesburrow Productions (USA), PenFro and Parthian Books (Wales), Fish Publishing (Ireland), Reflex Fiction, Between These Shores Books, Lapidus International, and Short Story Society (UK), KSP WriteFree Women's Writing Group, Busybird Publishing, Making Magic Happen Press, and Serenity Press (Australia).

Karen McDermott, you continue to be my lighthouse, mentoring me through rocky moments and pushing me to surf waves bigger than I ever dreamt possible. I extend my thanks also for inviting me into your beautiful inner circle of authors who all offer daily encouragement and friendship. To those inside this circle, together we are an unstoppable herd of unicorns.

Karen Sanders, our chats are endless, and I would not have it any other way. Thanks for delving into my weird and wonderful world and putting my work into the spotlight on your Ageing Fearlessly Podcasts and radio show…and inviting me back again for more!

The Adecco Group, you are truly an organisation who support working parents and diversity, promoting work life balance and allowing voices for change to flourish. To my colleagues across the global business who have stood behind my mad literary projects, thank you for letting me live by my values and write about issues I am passionate about. The future is ours to shape.

KSP wonder women, Lisa Wolstenholme, Elizabeth Lewis, and Shannon Coyle, I will never forget being in my writing bubble in the Perth Hills and everything I gained from being awarded a First Edition Fellowship. Many of the short stories in this collection were created in that Western Australia sanctuary. To all at the Society of Women Writers in NSW, it is a true delight to expand my network on the east coast and to keep learning and growing with you all.

Tess Woods, the first story I wrote for this collection was published from an introduction you facilitated and the rest is history – I figure I still owe you a Pimms. There are so many other amazing authors and poets who have shared advice and support, providing constant inspiration to keep pushing the boundaries. The writing community I belong to is one huge extended family and I will be forever grateful for being made welcome. I am also indebted to every blogger, reviewer, book seller, event organiser, and journalist who has showcased my work. Thank you to the readers of my written word, listeners of my spoken slams, and viewers of my poetry movies and TV segments; my amplified voice would be reduced to a whisper without you.

To my tribe of friends who instinctively reach out when I hit a rough patch, make me laugh when I want to cry, and back me to the hilt, I would be one lonely chick without you. Jacqui, Jacki, Vez, Laura, Grace, Angela, and Emma, thanks for truly knowing and accepting my rawness beneath the make-up.

To the Hendersons, Doubells, and Van Nelsons, thanks for believing in me decades before I ever got my lucky break. From the different corners of the earth we all live in, we stay connected and supportive as a family and that's what it's all about.

Lastly, endless thanks from the bottom of my heart to Shaun, Kayin, and Imani. Every day I sleep with greater peace, love with deeper ferocity, and write with more conviction because of you. These are my purest truths in a book packed with muddy fiction.

Lightning Source UK Ltd.
Milton Keynes UK
UKHW010647131221
395574UK00001B/47

9 781761 090387